CW00539933

SHIELDING JAYME

Delta Team Two, Book 4

SUSAN STOKER

Edited by Kelli Collins

Cover Design by AURA Design Group

Manufactured in the United States

CHAPTER ONE

"You're acting weird, Memaw, what's up?" Jayme
Caldwell asked, eyeing her grandmother with suspi-
cion. Winnie Morrison was one of Jayme's favorite
people in the world. She was ninety-one years old but
acted like a woman thirty years younger. She was a
busy-body, but no one got upset with her for butting
into their business because she was so nice about it.
She never met a stranger, and it wasn't unlike her to
invite said strangers to her house for a cup of tea.

Jayme had moved down to Killeen, Texas, to live
with her grandmother while she decided what she
wanted to do with her life. She thought she'd found,
or been building a perfect life in Seattle, but that
hadn't worked out...and it was also the reason she was
now floundering trying to figure out what to do next.

1

"Nothing's up," Winnie said, not quite meeting Jayme's eye.

Sighing, Jayme decided not to push. She'd find out soon enough what had her grandmother acting so odd. She kept looking down at her phone and smiling. Jayme had bought her the iPhone a year and a half ago so she could more easily keep in touch with their family, and she was worse than a teenager; constantly checking her texts and sending crazy memes to all her friends.

"Is dinner still going to be ready at six?" Winnie asked.

"Yup. Why, got a hot date?" Jayme teased. She'd offered to make dinner for her memaw. She loved cooking, but hadn't had a chance lately to go all out. But tonight was the night. She'd prepared Caesar salad with homemade dressing, spinach artichoke dip with crackers, chicken parmesan stuffed shells, and her specialty Butterfinger cake for dessert. Of course, she also couldn't resist making a loaf of banana bread, as well as Memaw's favorite...old fashioned peanut butter cookies.

Baking made everything seem right in Jayme's world...even when it was actually falling apart around her. When she was in the kitchen, all her stress seemed to fall away...and she could forget for a while why she'd moved to Texas to live with her grandmother.

"It smells delicious in here, love," Winnie said as she came up beside Jayme and put her arm around her. Jayme wasn't tall, but even at only five-five, she towered over her memaw. Winnie was only five-one but because of her outgoing personality, she seemed a lot taller.

"Thanks," Jayme said, flushing with pride. One of her favorite things in the world was feeding people. It satisfied something deep within her.

"Why don't you go upstairs and change," Winnie suggested.

"Change?" Jayme asked in confusion, looking down at herself. She had on a pair of jeans and a T-shirt. The apron over her clothes was covered in flour and other smears of food. She wasn't the neatest cook, but no one had ever complained after they'd tasted what she'd made.

"Yeah. Maybe put on that sundress you were wearing when you got here. It's cute and looks great on you."

Jayme wrinkled her brow. "But it's just us. Why would I dress up?"

Her memaw shrugged. "I don't know, why not? I put on one of my favorite dresses."

Jayme nodded. She hadn't wanted to ask her

grandmother why she'd gussied up; she was eccentric on her best days. And she supposed it wouldn't hurt to change. She'd learned over the years that it was easier to humor her memaw than argue with her.

Wiping her hands, Jayme put the dishtowel down on the counter and headed for the stairs to her bedroom. Winnie didn't have a lot of space in her house, but that suited her just fine. She had a house-cleaner who came in once a week to help keep things clean and tidy, and she'd said more than once that she didn't need a huge house. Then she'd winked and told Jayme that if she ever moved, she'd no longer be able to ogle the hot Army soldier who regularly mowed her lawn.

Jayme shook her head as she took off her shirt and jeans. Her grandmother was hilarious, and she dreaded the time when she wouldn't be in her life anymore. No one understood her like Memaw did. Not even her parents.

Jayme had already tried to explain to her mom how she felt about what had happened back in Seattle, but Mom didn't understand what the big deal was.

After slipping the red sundress with white polka dots over her head, she sat on the edge of her bed and sighed.

Thinking about the bakery that she'd thought

4

would be hers one day was depressing. She'd worked her ass off at The Gingerbread House for a decade. Jayme had been assured that when the owner retired, she was going to sell it to her. Claire was a sweet old woman who loved baking as much as Jayme did.

But three months ago, she'd pulled Jayme aside and informed her that her nephew would be taking over the bakery.

Shaking her head and trying to banish the thoughts of how horrible the last three months had been, Jayme stood and went into the bathroom in the hallway. Staring at her reflection, she couldn't help but wince. She looked rough. Her cheeks were pale and the dark circles under her eyes made it clear that she wasn't sleeping well. Her light brown locks were in disarray, having been thrown up in a messy bun to keep them out of her face while she cooked.

Jayme took out the scrunchie and quickly brushed her hair. It was thick, and most of the time a pain in the butt to deal with. The ends curled around her breasts, which Jayme thought were too big for her frame. The sundress hugged her curves as well, making her a little uncomfortable, but since it would just be her and her grandmother tonight, Jayme left off the wrap she usually wore to try to hide behind.

Standing up straight, Jayme took a deep breath. She wasn't exactly ready to walk a red carpet, but she begrudgingly admitted the dress was flattering. Jayme was working on her self-confidence, in all aspects of her life. Losing the chance to own her own bakery had been a blow to her self-esteem. She was a damn good baker, and cook, and was happy to spend as much time with her memaw as she could.

Not bothering to put on makeup—she was drawing a line there—Jayme turned and headed for the stairs once more. She needed to check on the stuffed shells and stir the dressing. The smell of freshly baked cookies permeated the air, making Jayme smile as she headed for the kitchen.

Stopping in her tracks at the edge of the small room, Jayme blinked in confusion.

Her memaw was in the kitchen—along with a man Jayme had never seen before.

"Oh, here she is!" Memaw said brightly. "Come in and meet Rocket, love."

Rocket? Jayme was immediately confused, but she stepped forward politely.

"This is Rocket Long. I met him at the grocery store, and he was kind enough to help me to my car with all my parcels. He works on the Army base here as a helicopter mechanic. He's stopped by a few times to see how I'm getting along."

Looking up at the tall man standing beside her

grandmother, Jayme had to force herself not to turn tail and run.

He was absolutely gorgeous.

At least a foot taller than her, the man had black hair with a bit of gray at the temples and a sexy five o'clock shadow. His lips were full and currently quirked upward in a small smile. He had a square jaw, brown eyes the color of semi-sweet chocolate...and he smelled delicious. Like citrus. She assumed it was either his shampoo or his soap. Whatever it was, it made her want to bury her nose in the crook of his neck.

"Um...hi," Jayme said a little shyly, feeling intimidated by the good-looking man.

"And this is my granddaughter, Jayme Caldwell. She just moved here from Seattle. She's an amazing baker. Just wait until you taste her pastries. They're to die for."

"It's nice to meet you," Rocket said with a nod in her direction.

Jayme gave him a small smile, feeling immensely uncomfortable. She was great with strangers when she was working, not hesitating to offer suggestions as to what treat to try and explaining the ingredients in the delicacies she made, but socially, she'd always been awkward. Never knowing what to say or do around people she'd just met.

Memaw's phone trilled with the chime she'd downloaded for her text messages. Looking at her phone, she frowned. "Oh, dear," she said.

"What, what's wrong?" Jayme asked, concerned.

"Nothing. I just forgot that I said I'd go with Maude to bingo tonight. She's here now to pick me up. I'm so sorry, love. Rocket, you'll stay and keep my granddaughter company, won't you? She made this big meal and it shouldn't go to waste."

Jayme's face flamed. Darn it. She *knew* her memaw'd had something up her sleeve. Asking her to change into her sundress, to fix a grand meal for them tonight. She'd totally set this up! There was no way she'd forgotten about bingo with her friend. Winnie had a mind like a steel trap. She might be old, but her mind was as sharp as ever.

"Well, I—"

"She worked on dinner all afternoon," Winnie said, not letting Rocket graciously get out of the meal. "I'll be back by nine or ten. Don't wait up!"

Then she put a hand on Jayme's arm and stood on tiptoe to kiss her on the cheek. "Have fun," she whispered, winked, then turned and headed for the front door without a backward glance.

Jayme pressed her lips together and took a deep breath. She turned to the man still standing in her memaw's kitchen, looking out of place and completely dwarfing his surroundings. He smiled at her, and Jayme almost melted right there. The man was way too good-looking for her own good.

"You don't have to stay," she assured him. "If you're hungry, I can package some food up for you, but as someone who's been on the receiving end of Memaw's machinations too many times to count, I know how it feels to be blindsided by her."

"Is your cooking as good as Winnie claims?" Rocket asked.

Jayme wasn't conceited. Didn't like to brag. But she knew she was a good cook and baker. She shrugged and simply said, "Yes."

"Then if you aren't too uncomfortable to eat with a stranger, I'd love to stay."

CHAPTER TWO

Rocket stared silently at the woman in front of him and waited with bated breath to see what she'd say in response to his request to stay. He should be upset that Winnie had totally set them up. She hadn't mentioned that her granddaughter was in town when she'd texted and invited him over to eat last week.

He'd met Winnie a couple months ago at the grocery store, and surprisingly, they'd hit it off. She reminded him a lot of his own late grandmother. They'd exchanged phone numbers, and he'd been by her place a few times to check on her. Rocket missed his grandmother a lot—and he wasn't ashamed to admit that he was lonely.

He'd tried the dating thing. But none of the women he'd met had seemed to be interested in a long-term relationship. He was mostly content with his own company, but couldn't deny that Winnie was a breath of fresh air. She made him laugh and he liked that she seemed to enjoy his company as well.

He was single, hadn't been in a relationship with a woman in a few years, and the chance to have a home-cooked meal was too tempting to resist. Rocket wasn't very skilled in the kitchen. He didn't starve, thanks to his grill and frozen meals, but he'd learned over the years that his culinary abilities left a lot to be desired.

The second he'd stepped into Winnie's house tonight, his mouth had immediately started to water. It smelled absolutely divine. His stomach had growled, and he'd chuckled when Winnie raised an eyebrow at hearing it.

The last thing he wanted to do was go back to his empty house and nuke another microwaveable meal. He hoped Jayme would decide she was comfortable with him staying. Rocket knew he wasn't the most approachable-looking man. He was big. Tall and thick. He had to shop at specialty stores to get clothes that fit.

Shuffling where he was standing, he put his hands in his pockets to try to look less threatening. Most of the time he didn't mind the nervous glances people gave him. He wasn't much for idle chatter, and if people were scared of him, that meant they didn't try to engage him in conversation.

Winnie had been the rare exception. She'd gladly taken up his tentative offer to help get her groceries to her car and had babbled on, not seeming to care that he hadn't said much in response. Her grand-daughter clearly wasn't as talkative, though Rocket could see the physical similarities between Winnie and her granddaughter. Both were petite, had the same heart-shaped face, they even both had a slight dimple when they smiled. And he supposed before Winnie's hair went gray, she probably had the same light brown locks as Jayme.

Rocket did his best to keep his eyes on Jayme's face...but his mind was stuck on her curves. The red dress she had on lovingly outlined wide hips and an abundant chest. As a large man, Rocket had always been drawn to women who didn't look like they'd break if he touched them. She was lush...and his hands almost itched to see if her skin was as soft as it looked. Her dress fell to her knees, and for just a second, he imagined kneeling in front of her, running his hand under the hem. Up her thigh, hearing her breath catch in her throat, smelling her arousal as his hand got closer and closer to her soaking wet core...

"Any friend of Memaw's is a friend of mine," Jayme said softly.

And that voice. Just the sound of it made Rocket long for things he'd never had. Lazy nights cuddled together in his king-size bed, long intellectual conversations across the dinner table, hearing her whisper in his ear as he took her long, slow, and tenderly.

Shit. Clearly he'd been spending too much time alone. He had to stop thinking about sex, otherwise he was going to scare the shit out of Jayme with his hard-on.

When most people looked at him, they saw his size, his large hands, blackened with years of oil stains. They also assumed he wasn't all that bright, for some reason. But Rocket actually had a master's degree in business. He'd earned it from an online university—and hadn't told a soul. He'd been bored, wanted to challenge himself.

"It smells great in here," Rocket said, trying to put Jayme at ease.

She smiled, and it lit up her face. "Thanks."

"What are we having?" Rocket's mouth watered as she rattled off the menu. "Can I do anything to help?"

"Set the table?" Jayme asked.

Letting out a sigh of relief that she hadn't asked him to do anything related to cooking, Rocket nodded.

"Plates are in that cabinet, and the silverware is in that drawer over there."

Rocket stepped farther into the kitchen—and immediately realized how small the space was. He could smell Jayme's perfume, or lotion, or shampoo. She smelled like the beach, coconut and something tropical. He felt his dick twitch in his jeans and he willed himself to calm the fuck down. The very last thing he wanted to do was make her uncomfortable.

As he stepped closer to her, Rocket noted how short she was compared to him. He and Winnie had laughed at their extreme differences in height, and he'd gotten used to towering over most people. But looking at Jayme right now, it seemed they would actually fit together perfectly. If he took her in his arms, her head would rest against his chest.

The thought of holding her against him and burying his face in her hair made his muscles clench. This visceral reaction he was having to the woman was almost frightening.

"Are you all right?" Jayme asked in concern.

Rocket nodded. He needed to get his shit together. Otherwise Jayme was going to think he was a freak and warn her grandmother away from him. "Just hungry, I guess," he said with a smile.

"Good. I went overboard, like usual. There's enough food here for an army."

Rocket reached over her for the plates in the cabinet and headed toward the small table next to the kitchen before he did something stupid...like pull Jayme into his embrace.

"I'm really sorry Memaw tricked you," she said as she peered into the oven to check on the pasta.

"I'm not," Rocket said honestly. When he looked over, he saw Jayme blushing. He couldn't remember the last time he'd seen an honest-to-God blush on a woman's face. "Winnie's told me a bit about you. It's nice to meet you in person."

Jayme rolled her eyes. "Of course she has. Memaw can't resist telling her life story, and mine too, to everyone."

"She had nothing but good things to say," Rocket reassured her.

Jayme smiled. "She drives me crazy, but I love her. I don't know what I would've done if she hadn't invited me down here to Texas to stay with her for a while."

"Everything all right?" Rocket asked, wanting to know as much as possible about the woman. He got the silverware out of the drawer as she began to dish the Caesar salad into bowls.

She sighed. "Not really."

Rocket would have loved to tell her that he'd help however he could, but they'd just met. There was no reason for her to spill her guts to him or to accept any offer of assistance. "I know you don't know me...but I've been told I'm a good listener."

He took the bowls of salad from her, and she tilted her head up and looked into his eyes for a long moment. "Thanks," she said softly.

Rocket nodded. And while he was disappointed she hadn't taken him up on the offer to confide in him, he wasn't completely surprised.

The next few minutes was spent getting the food to the table. Then Rocket held Jayme's chair for her, and she thanked him quietly again as she sat.

"This looks incredible," Rocket said in awe.

"It's nothing special," Jayme replied a little self-consciously.

"Wrong. It's amazing. I can't remember the last time I had a home-cooked meal that looked as good as this," Rocket told her.

"Well, leave room for dessert, because I've been told my Butterfinger cake is to die for."

Rocket groaned.

"And I made some peanut butter cookies for Memaw, but after her shenanigans tonight, I think I'm gonna give them all to you to take home."

"Will you marry me?" Rocket blurted.

Jayme laughed—and Rocket realized he'd only been half-kidding. He didn't know anything about this woman except that she was a hell of a cook. But simply being around her made him feel lighter. Happier. More content.

"Perhaps I'll just be your cookie dealer," she returned.

"Done," Rocket said without hesitation.

"Maybe you shouldn't commit before you taste everything," she said with a small shrug.

"I don't have to. Anything you make will be one hundred percent better than what I can whip up myself."

"You don't cook?" she asked as she picked up her fork.

Following her lead, Rocket speared some of his salad and took a bite, swallowing before he answered. "Nope. Not at all. Never learned the basics growing up. My mom wasn't around, and my dad's idea of dinner was to slap some bologna between two pieces of bread and call it done. When we could afford it, we splurged on takeout."

Instead of looking at him with pity, Jayme seemed more curious. "You never learned as an adult?"

Rocket shrugged. "When I graduated from high school, I joined the Navy. Spent a lot of time on ships in the middle of the ocean. Food was always provided for me. Since I got out and started working for contractors, I've been content to live on takeout and frozen meals."

"Memaw said you were a helicopter mechanic?" Jayme asked.

Rocket nodded. He didn't really like to talk about himself, but he'd tell this woman anything she wanted to know. "Yeah. I helped my dad rebuild cars when I was in high school, and it seemed like a natural progression when I joined the Navy. I didn't like the military life, but I loved tinkering with engines. So now I get to do what I love, but I don't have to deal with the rules and regulations that come with being a sailor."

"That's great," Jayme said.

"So is this," Rocket told her, nodding to the stuffed shells he was eating. "Seriously, I've never tasted anything so good."

"Thanks," she said shyly.

"Have you always wanted to be a cook?"

"Not a cook, but a baker, yes," she said.

"There's a difference?" Rocket asked.

She chuckled. "Yeah. The differences lie in the kind of products they make. Bakers primarily make breads, cookies, cakes, pastries, and other baked goods. Chefs don't focus on one kind of food, but make all sorts of different meals."

Rocket looked down at his empty plate and then back up at Jayme. "Seems to me that you're both."

She was still smiling. "Well, I like to cook, but I

love to bake."

"Then I can't wait to taste those cookies and your Butterfinger cake," Rocket said.

An hour later, after four cookies and two helpings of the most amazing cake he'd ever eaten, Rocket was sitting with Jayme in Winnie's living room. She was holding a cup of tea, and she'd brewed a pot of coffee for him. He was full, and feeling extremely content to sit and chat with one of the most interesting women he'd met in a very long time.

"So, you never did say what brought you to Texas," Rocket started, desperate to learn more about Jayme.

She shrugged and looked into her teacup. "It's not a very interesting story."

"To me it is," Rocket said simply.

"Why?"

Why indeed. He slowly leaned over and put his coffee cup on the table in front of him and waited for Jayme to look up. When she finally met his gaze, he said, "I came over tonight expecting, after a nice meal with Winnie, to go back to my house and spend the rest of the night alone. Just as I have every other night of my life. I get up, go to work, go home, watch TV, sleep...then do it again the next day. I don't have a lot of friends, and people are generally wary of me because of my size.

"You had every right to be upset with Winnie for setting us up; you could've told me you weren't comfortable being alone with me, but instead, you fed me the best meal I've had in years and you haven't treated me as if I might be dangerous or violent just because of my size. You're also beautiful...and I can't understand why you aren't married with a houseful of children by now. The men in your life must all be complete idiots.

"I want to know more about you, Jayme. I don't know why I'm so drawn to you, maybe part of it is because you took pity on a hungry bachelor, but I am. You probably think I'm a creeper now, and that sucks, but if I left here without letting you know I've had a wonderful evening so far, and that I'd like to see you again, take you out on a date, I'd never forgive myself. So...yeah, everything about you is interesting to me. Including how you ended up here."

The second he stopped speaking, and she remained silent, Rocket wanted to kick himself.

He was an idiot. He'd never been all that good in social situations, and this was why. He tended to say what he was thinking, even if it made him look like a weirdo.

Still berating himself, he held his breath as he waited for Jayme's response.

CHAPTER THREE

Jayme stared at the man sitting nearby. He was in the easy chair her grandpa had always sat in, leaning forward, his elbows resting on his knees, his eyes focused on her.

She hated to learn that people treated him badly simply because of his size. Interestingly, she hadn't been leery of him at all. Even though he was a foot taller and outweighed her by at least a hundred pounds. Maybe it was because Memaw trusted him. Maybe it was because of the way he looked at her grandmother with respect.

"I'm sorry I made you uncomfortable. I'll head on out now," Rocket said after she remained silent too long. He shifted to stand.

Jayme's hand shot out before she could think

about what she was doing. She touched his thigh, just above his knee and he froze comically, half-standing, half-sitting.

"Stay," Jayme said quickly.

Rocket slowly lowered himself back into the chair, and Jayme could feel his muscles under her hand shifting as he moved. She licked her lips and reluctantly took her hand off his leg and gripped her teacup once again.

It had been a long time since a man had intrigued her as much as Rocket. He looked nothing like the men she'd dated in the past. He wasn't as refined. Was more...wild. Rougher. But she liked that about him.

Swallowing hard, she said, "I was an idiot. That's why I'm here."

"I don't believe that for a second," Rocket said without hesitation.

"Thanks, but I was. I worked at a small bakery out in Seattle for ten years. The owner, Claire, was an older woman who reminded me a lot of my memaw in so many ways. When I first started working at The Gingerbread House, she was my mentor. She taught me a lot about owning a business. We would get to work at four-thirty and spend the time before the doors opened baking and laughing. She knew me better than anyone else. She was like a second mother to me."

Jayme stopped and took a sip of her tea, wishing she didn't feel as if she was on the verge of tears. She should be angry about what happened, but instead she was heartbroken.

Rocket didn't push her to continue. He didn't rush her at all. When Jayme glanced over, she saw his eyes were focused on her. He wasn't fidgeting or looking bored. It was a heady feeling to be the center of this man's attention.

"Anyway, over the years, things slowly started to change. Claire didn't come to work in the mornings until we'd been open for an hour or so. More and more of the everyday operations fell to me. I was okay with that though, because I was under the assumption that the store would be mine someday. Claire and I had talked about it, and she'd told me that when she was ready to retire, she'd sell the store to me."

Jayme stopped talking again, but this time it was because her throat had closed up. Thinking about what happened was as painful now as it had been three months ago...the day Claire had said she needed to talk to her.

Jayme felt the cushion next to her depress, and

the next thing she knew, Rocket was sitting next to her. He took the cup out of her hands and placed it on the coffee table. Then he took both her hands in his and simply held them lightly.

She could smell his citrusy scent, and she had a feeling she'd never smell lemons again and not think of this man. "I'm okay," she whispered.

"Take your time," Rocket told her gently.

It took another few moments before she could speak again. "I was doing most of the work at the store. I was in charge of all the employees, ordering supplies, making sure everything got baked in the mornings. So when Claire asked to speak to me, I was sure she was going to tell me that she was retiring and wanted to discuss terms to sell the store. But instead, she told me that her nephew would be taking over. That she was selling The Gingerbread House to *him*.

"I was so shocked. Her nephew had only been in the bakery a few times that I knew of in the entire time I'd worked there. She apologized and told me she hoped I stayed on as manager. She wanted me to teach her nephew the ropes.

"It hurt. Bad. I'd put a decade of blood, sweat, and tears into that bakery, only to have my hopes and dreams ripped out from under me. Still, I didn't want to let Claire down. I tried. I really did. But her nephew is an idiot. He doesn't care about the bakery or the loyal customers. All he wants is money. He fired a few of the staff and cut so many corners, the tried-and-true pastries we'd offered for so many years no longer tasted the same because of the generic ingredients he insisted we start using. I couldn't take it any longer and finally quit.

"I couldn't bear to stay in Seattle after that, so I asked Memaw if I could come stay with her a while until I figured out what I wanted to do with my life."

"I'm sorry," Rocket said.

Jayme appreciated his simple but heartfelt sympathy. "Me too."

"This might be overstepping my bounds here, but as someone who's appreciated your culinary talents firsthand...why don't you open your own bakery?"

Jayme studied him. She was all too aware he hadn't let go of her hands, and she wasn't in any hurry to have him do so. "I've thought about it, but it's a lot of work."

"And operating The Gingerbread House wasn't?" Rocket countered. "It seems to me that the best things in life are those that are the hardest to obtain. You said you were practically running that bakery in Washington by yourself. Managing the staff, ordering the supplies, actually baking the goods...you already know how hard the job is and what's involved."

Jayme bit her lip. She *did* know. She'd put her

heart and soul into that bakery in Seattle and when it had been taken from her, she'd grieved. But it had been months now, and she was officially bored. She loved her memaw, but she needed to *do* something.

"I'm sorry, I'm sure you've already thought of the ins and outs of this," Rocket said, loosening his hand.

Jayme tightened her fingers around his, refusing to let him pull away. "I think I'm just scared. What if I fail?"

"Then you find something else to do," Rocket said, simply and without judgement. "But for the record, if tonight's desserts were anything to go by, you aren't going to fail. In fact, I think if you find a place right here in Killeen, you'll succeed beyond your wildest imagination. There are a lot of guys like me—single and with a horrible sweet tooth—who would love to be able to get some homemade goodies whenever we wanted. And not just guys, of course; I'm sure women would bend over backward for some wholesome treats too."

Jayme appreciated his encouragement. "I've got some awesome low-calorie recipes too."

Rocket grinned, then got serious. "I'm sorry you were disappointed by your friend. I don't know this Claire person, but I'm sure she's regretting what she did. Her nephew has probably run her precious bakery into the ground by now. But don't let her actions ruin *your* dream. You can be grateful to her for giving you the opportunity to learn what you needed to learn to run your own business, while still feeling hurt over her actions."

That was true. Jayme still had mixed feelings about what had happened. She loved Claire, but had been so very hurt over what she'd done. "Thanks," she said softly.

"You're gonna need a kick-ass name for your bakery though," Rocket said. "What about Pie in the Sky?"

Jayme grinned and wrinkled her nose.

"No? What about, Holy Cannoli?"

She laughed outright at that. "Uh, no."

"Right, too corny. It needs to be something that encompasses more than just cakes, cookies, or bread, so you can't have any of those words in the name. You don't want people thinking all you make is bread or cookies or whatever, but it can't be so broad that no one knows what the business is."

"You seem to know a lot about this kind of thing," Jayme noted.

Rocket shrugged. "I have a master's degree in business. Took a class on marketing."

"You do? Really?"

"I know, a mechanic having a master's degree is surprising," he said self-deprecatingly.

"No, it isn't that," Jayme said quickly, not wanting him to think she was dissing him in any way. "I just... most people don't understand this stuff. When I tried to talk to Memaw about it, she didn't really understand how much work goes into owning a business. She means well, but she thinks all I need to do is make a bunch of cookies and they'll sell without any effort."

"Nothing about owning a business is easy," Rocket said. "I would've started my own business, but helicopter repair isn't exactly high in demand with the general population."

Jayme chuckled. "Right, until we all have helicopters in our garages I can see why working for a contractor is the best move for you."

He returned her smile. "What names have you thought of for your bakery? And don't tell me you haven't thought of any, because I won't believe you."

How did this man know her so well after only a few hours? "Promise you won't laugh?" she asked.

"I'd never laugh at you," he said seriously.

Jayme believed him. It was crazy, but something about this man made her want to believe her dream could come true. "Confection Connection?"

Rocket wrinkled his nose.

"Yeah, that wasn't my first choice," Jayme agreed. "What about Dream Puffs? Or The Baker's Table?"

"Better, but I'm not sure they really fit *you*."

"Warm Delights?" Jayme asked, holding her breath. That had been her favorite of all the names she'd come up with.

"Warm Delights...I like it. It gives the impression of all sorts of treats, not just cookies or pies. And if you ever wanted to branch out and do more than desserts, you could sell pot pies, casseroles, things like that."

Jayme beamed. "That's what I thought too. Rocket...?"

"Yeah?"

"I'm not scared of you." As surprise registered on his face, more words came tumbling out of her. She'd been thinking about what he'd said earlier and she wanted—no *needed* him to know that she didn't think he'd ever hurt her. "Most of the men I've dated haven't understood that baking calms me. That being in the kitchen is what fills my soul. They haven't understood that I'd rather spend an evening baking than going to a music concert or to the movies. I was an annoying kid; just as my grandmother, she'll tell you so many stories about how I wouldn't stop bugging her or my mother to show me how to use some new kitchen utensil, or how I hated to play outside because I'd rather be inside with them baking or cooking. So now you know what my dream for the future is, owning my own bakery—and I don't think you're a creeper."

Jayme was almost panting by the time she got done with her little speech, but she'd rushed through it so she wouldn't chicken out. She was more content to fade into the background and not bring attention to herself, so telling Rocket what she really thought had been hard...but the smile on his face was worth all the angst she'd built up inside before she'd finally shared her thoughts.

"Good. Can I take you on a date?"

"I'd like that," Jayme said shyly. "I haven't seen much of Killeen yet."

Rocket grinned. "I'd be honored to show you around."

"Cool."

"Cool," he echoed.

Then he surprised her by sitting back on the couch but not letting go of her hand. "I could leave now, but that would deprive Winnie of the satisfaction of knowing how well we got along...and how well her little plan worked."

Jayme laughed. "Right? Although she probably deserves to be disappointed and think her scheming didn't work for a while."

"Do you really care?" Rocket asked.

Did she? No. She loved her memaw, and while it was a little embarrassing to be set up by her, if things worked out between her and Rocket, she couldn't really be too mad. "No," she told him.

"Me either. I don't suppose Winnie's got cable?" he asked skeptically.

Jayme laughed. "Not only does she have cable, she has Netflix, Hulu, Amazon Prime, and Apple TV."

Rocket's eyes widened. "Seriously?"

"Yup. She says that she needs to stay up on what's hip in the world," Jayme told him.

"Your grandmother's cooler than I am," Rocket said.

"Me too," Jayme agreed as she reached for the remote and clicked on the television.

She had no idea how much time had passed while they watched a British reality series about a helicopter 9-1-1 unit, but Jayme realized she'd fallen asleep when she heard voices speaking around her.

Opening her eyes, she saw that Rocket had turned off the lights...and she'd somehow snuggled herself almost onto his lap. His arm was around her, and she was using his shoulder as a pillow. He'd covered her up with a blanket, and she felt warm and safe in his arms.

He shifted next to her, and Jayme felt herself

being lowered to the cushions. "I'll call you tomorrow," Rocket told her softly.

Jayme nodded. She was having a hard time keeping her eyes open.

"Go back to sleep," Rocket told her. "I'll see myself out."

"Rocket?"

"Yeah?"

"I had a good time tonight."

"Me too."

Then she felt his warm lips against her forehead before she sensed him moving away. She heard more low conversation, probably Rocket saying goodbye to Memaw, before she heard her grandmother shuffling back into the room. Knowing she needed to get up and go to her bedroom, Jayme slowly sat upright, keeping the blanket that smelled like Rocket around her shoulders.

"It looks like you had a good time tonight," Memaw said with a devilish grin.

"I did," Jayme told her. "How was bingo?"

"Annoying. I hate that stupid game."

"Then why do you keep going?"

"Because. I'm going to win one of these times, I just know it," her grandmother said.

Jayme could only shake her head in exasperation.

"So, Rocket's gonna call you tomorrow?"

"You ever hear of privacy?" Jayme asked.

"Nope. I assume you guys clicked?"

"Yeah, Memaw, we clicked," Jayme told her.

"I knew you would!" her grandmother crowed.

"Yeah, well, we aren't getting married, so slow your roll."

Winnie threw her head back and laughed. "*Yet.* I want to give you away," her grandmother said.

Jayme could only shake her head in exasperation. "That's such an archaic tradition."

"Don't care. Your daddy didn't have anything to do with you meeting Rocket. That was all me. So I want to be the one to give you to him."

"Fine. If we get married, I'll let you walk me down the aisle. Happy?"

"Immensely. But you can't wait too long. I'm not getting any younger," Memaw quipped.

She'd been saying that for as long as Jayme could remember to try to get her way. "We haven't even been on a date, Memaw. We might find out that we don't really get along."

"Hogwash. Looked like the two of you were more than getting along when I walked in."

Jayme knew she was blushing.

"Did he like your chicken parmesan stuffed shells?"

"Yes."

"And your cookies, bread, and Butterfinger pie?"

"Yes."

"Right. There ya go. There's no better way to a man's heart than through his stomach. That man doesn't cook for himself, so all you gotta do is feed him and you'll have him snared."

"I don't want to snare him," Jayme said quietly. "I want a man who likes me for who I am, not because I can feed him."

"Who you are is a baker," her grandmother said gently. "From the moment you first held a spatula in your hand, that's all you were interested in. Finding a man who appreciates that about you is a blessing. You've told me yourself how many men you've dated don't understand that about you. I had a feeling about Rocket when I first met him. He's lonely. He's not a man who likes to go out on the town or party. He owns his own house, did he tell you that?"

"No," Jayme said.

"He does. Bought it a while ago because he wanted to live someplace quiet. Said he didn't want to live in an apartment, have to worry about someone else burning down his home because they'd left a candle burning. He had the kitchen and bathrooms done up all fancy too, in the hopes he might find a woman who wouldn't mind spending her nights holed up with him."

"It's rude to talk about someone behind their back," Jayme protested.

"Fine. I'm just sayin' that as I got to know that man, I couldn't help but think that you two would get on like peanut butter and jelly. And my instincts were right. Give him a chance, love."

"He asked me out," Jayme told her grandmother.

She beamed. "Good. You had better get up to bed and get some beauty rest."

Jayme resisted the urge to roll her eyes. "Yes, ma'am." She stood, keeping the blanket around her shoulders, and was halfway to the stairs in her grandma's small house when she heard Memaw say her name. Turning, Jayme looked back at her.

"Love you, child. Rocket's a good man. Give him a chance."

"I will," Jayme said softly.

Memaw nodded, and Jayme continued up the stairs. She lay in her bed for a long time, staring up at the ceiling. It felt a little weird being set up by her grandmother, but she couldn't deny the sparks between her and Rocket.

She had no idea where things between them would go, but she was looking forward to talking to him the next day. And she was thankful that she'd decided to come to Texas to figure her life out. She hadn't planned on meeting a man, but now that she'd met Rocket, she wasn't so interested in moving anywhere else.

She hadn't felt this much excitement about a relationship in a very long time, and Jayme couldn't wait to see what the future held.

CHAPTER FOUR

Rocket took a deep breath and tried to calm his racing heart as he drove toward Winnie's house to pick up Jayme for another date. Over the last two weeks, he'd talked to her every day and he'd seen her three times. He'd have preferred to see her more, but his schedule was hectic, and because of events overseas, he'd been working long hours on the Army base's helicopters to keep them running in tip-top shape.

But he'd gotten the afternoon off, and he'd planned something pretty over-the-top for their date today. He wasn't sure how Jayme would feel about it though, so he was taking a chance.

He'd taken her out to eat once and their conversation had felt a bit stilted. He'd had a good time but hadn't been truly relaxed. And that sucked because he really liked Jayme. Wanted to see where things could go between them. Didn't want to fuck anything up. Jayme was pretty, practical, and he really liked how devoted she was to Winnie. He didn't have a close relationship with his own family, more his fault than anything his parents had done. He'd just gotten busy with his life and before he knew it, he hadn't seen his mom or dad in years.

The next time he'd taken Jayme out, he'd given her a driving tour of Killeen. He'd been a little more relaxed that time and things between them seemed more laid-back, more like when he'd eaten dinner with her at Winnie's. And on date three, Rocket had brought her onto the Army base and given her a tour of where he worked and introduced her to his coworkers.

He'd loved how down-to-earth she was and how she laughed and joked with his friends, not caring about shaking their oily hands or the fact that most of them were rough around the edges.

The more Rocket got to know Jayme, the more he liked her.

He pulled into Winnie's driveway and climbed out of his old Chevy Blazer. The car might be ancient, but she ran perfectly, thanks to his mechanical abilities. Rocket gave Winnie's next-door neighbor, Brain, a chin lift in greeting. The man was outside washing his girlfriend's car. He and Aspen had introduced themselves one day while he'd been visiting Winnie, and Rocket had to admit it made him feel better that her neighbors were watching out for her.

She might think she was perfectly able to look after herself, but at ninety-one, she was vulnerable. Aspen had also said recently that she was happy Jayme had moved in so she could help keep an eye on the spunky older woman.

Jogging up to the door, Rocket lifted his hand to knock but it opened before he could make contact.

"Hey," Jayme said, smiling up at him.

And just like that, Rocket's day was made.

"Hi," he returned, leaning down without thought. One of his hands rested on her bicep and he brushed his lips against her cheek in greeting.

She blushed, but her smile never dimmed.

"You ready to go?" he asked.

"Yup. Memaw left about half an hour ago for lunch with one of her friends. The senior bus picked her up."

Rocket nodded. "I think it's great that she's still getting out and about so much."

Jayme rolled her eyes. "If she didn't, she'd be a pain in the ass. She needs her gossip time. Hang on a sec, let me grab my purse." She ducked back inside the house and Rocket waited patiently on the front step. Today was his day off, and two weeks ago he would've been doing yard work or puttering around his garage, working on the old Harley he'd picked up a while ago.

She was back in less than a minute, and when she turned around to lock the front door, Rocket couldn't help but let his eyes stray to her ass. The woman had one of the finest backsides he'd ever seen, and it took everything he had not to reach out to touch her.

She turned and caught him staring, but instead of getting irritated, she simply chuckled. "You're such a guy," she said.

Rocket shrugged. "Guilty."

Her cheeks were pink, which made Rocket want her all the more. He knew she was thirty-two, but sometimes she reminded him of an untried teenager. He liked that she wasn't jaded and didn't flaunt her sexuality. She didn't need to. All she had to do was smile at him and he was putty in her hands.

"Now that we're on our way, are you finally going to tell me what we're doing today?" she asked.

"Nope. Not yet," Rocket said, amused that she was so easy to tease.

"Okay, but you should know that there's a freshly baked cheesecake waiting on Winnie's counter that I made this morning...and I'm still deciding if I'm gonna let you have any of it."

"Oh, you're cruel," Rocket said, holding a hand to his chest as he opened the passenger door to his truck with the other.

She chuckled. "Nope, you're the cruel one. I've been wracking my brain trying to figure out why all the secrecy for our date and where you might be taking me."

"I thought bakers were supposed to be patient," Rocket said as she got settled in his truck.

"Not this one," Jayme told him.

Rocket couldn't help himself, he brought a hand up to her hair and smoothed it back. She'd left it down, which he loved, and the thick locks curled around her shoulders, drawing his eyes to her chest. She had on a V-neck T-shirt that showed just a hint of cleavage. Her jeans molded to her legs, caressing her curves.

His mouth actually watered with his need to explore her, to peel off her shirt and worship her. "Hang on just a bit longer, my curious baker, and you'll see for yourself what I have planned. But know, if you hate it, plans can easily be changed."

Tilting her head, Jayme studied him. "You're nervous," she stated.

Rocket shrugged. "Yeah."

"Why?"

"Because I want you to have fun. I want to

impress you. The last thing I'd *ever* want to do it scare you." He sighed. "And I'm nervous because I like you, Jayme. I don't want to do anything that would make you second-guess going out with me."

She stared up at him for a long moment before saying, "You have nothing to be worried about, Rocket. I'm the one who's unemployed. Who's living off the generosity of her grandmother. You're...*you*," she used her hand to gesture toward him, "and I'm me." She shrugged. "Anyone who sees us together is probably wondering what the hell you're doing with me."

"Wrong," Rocket said immediately. "They're likely jealous as hell that I'm with you and they aren't. Buckle up." He stepped back before he did something stupid, like kiss the hell out of her. He hated that she was insecure. If anyone in this budding relationship should be insecure, it was him. He knew without a doubt that he'd hit the jackpot. And he'd do whatever it took to make sure she never wondered if she could do better than him.

He hurried around his truck and climbed behind the wheel. After he pulled out of the driveway, he looked over at Jayme. She was staring at him and smiling. "What?" he asked.

"Nothing. I'm just happy," she said. "I have no idea where we're going or what we're doing, but being around you is relaxing. I don't have to worry about getting lost or being harassed, or even what to say."

Without thought, Rocket reached for her hand, sighing in relief when she didn't hesitate to wrap her fingers around his own. "You never have to worry about those things when you're with me. You'll *always* be safe with me."

"I know," Jayme said softly. "Thank you."

He squeezed her hand in reply.

Within ten minutes, they were driving through the gates of Fort Hood and headed to the hangar where he worked.

"Did you forget to show me something when we were here last?" Jayme asked.

Rocket loved that she hadn't guessed his plans. "Not exactly," he told her. He parked his truck and took hold of her hand again as he led her toward a helicopter sitting out on the tarmac. He stopped a short distance from the machine and turned to her. "I thought I'd take you for a helicopter ride today."

Jayme's eyes widened. "Seriously?"

"Yeah. One of the pilots is doing a test ride today —don't worry, I got all the approvals I needed to take you up, and it's completely safe, I guarantee it. He just needs to test out of some of the fixes we've done on the engine. I wouldn't take you up in a bird that I didn't know was one hundred percent reliable."

"And you did the work on it?" Jayme asked.

Rocket nodded. "Yeah."

"Then I know it's safe," she said quietly.

Her instant confidence in his abilities made Rocket feel as if he was ten feet tall. "If you're scared or nervous, we don't have to do it. I just thought it might be a fun way for you to see more of the area. And get a free helicopter ride in the process."

"I've never been in one," Jayme told him, looking over at the chopper. "I'm nervous, but excited too." She looked back up at him. "Thank you. This is amazing."

Rocket relaxed a bit. "It's okay?"

"More than okay," Jayme told him. "And that cheesecake I threatened you with earlier?"

"Yeah?"

"It's all yours. And I'll even throw in the double chocolate chip cookies and the loaf of chocolate banana bread I made for Memaw too."

Rocket chuckled. "Awesome. Although you know you don't have to keep baking for me. I like you without the bribes."

"I want to. I tend to bake more when I'm happy. And I've been very happy in the last couple of weeks."

"Good." Rocket wanted to kiss her. *Really* kiss her. But he also knew the pilots of the chopper were watching. And the last thing he wanted to do was embarrass Jayme. But it was extremely difficult to do nothing more than smile down at her. "Come on, I can't wait to see what you think of your first helicopter ride."

Jayme couldn't stop smiling. She couldn't believe that Rocket had taken her for a freaking helicopter ride! He'd helped her settle into the chopper, and when his hands had brushed over her hips when he helped fasten her seat belt, her thighs had clenched together, hard.

She wanted this man. Badly. She'd never been someone who *needed* sex. She'd always thought she had a pretty low sex drive. But since meeting Rocket, she scarcely thought of anything else.

He was a big man...and she assumed that meant that he was big all over. If the old wives' tale about the size of a man's hands and feet being an indicator of the size of his dick was true, Jayme had a feeling she was going to have a hard time taking him. But oh, how she wanted to try.

Then Rocket had gently placed the headset over her head and adjusted the microphone so it sat in front of her lips, and she struggled to think about

SUSAN STOKER

anything other than pulling him down and kissing him.

Luckily, the pilot had asked him something, and he'd turned away to answer the question, so she'd been spared doing anything really embarrassing.

Rocket was one of the most amazing men she'd ever met. He'd gotten his master's degree online simply because he'd been bored. He'd rebuilt several cars and motorcycles almost from scratch, just for fun. Then there was how great he was with Memaw. It also seemed that everyone she met had nothing but the utmost respect for him.

Jayme had been a bit nervous when the helicopter first took off, and had probably left fingernail marks in Rocket's hand, but before too long, she'd relaxed enough to truly enjoy the flight. Rocket alternated between talking to the pilots about technical aspects of the flight and pointing out landmarks for her. They flew over Fort Hood, and she got to see exactly how large the Army base was. Over Interstate 35, she laughed when Rocket pointed out the best place for her bakery...near one of the gates of the post, but still far enough away for people not affiliated with the military to feel comfortable shopping.

He amazed her with his business acumen and his excitement for a business that was nothing but a dream at the moment.

Throughout the flight, he also held her hand, leaning over and pointing out landmarks, pressing his body against hers. His citrusy smell was driving her crazy, and it took everything she had not to turn and attack the poor man. The flight was probably only about twenty minutes or so, but it seemed as if they'd been in the air much longer, with Jayme ultra-aware of him for every second of the ride.

She was still smiling as Rocket drove them off the Army post.

"You liked that?" he asked.

"Duh," Jayme told him. "It was amazing! Exciting! Stupendous! Something I never thought I'd do in my lifetime."

"Good."

"What now? And I'm not sure how you can ever top that, by the way."

Rocket wrinkled his nose adorably. "True. Shit. Maybe I shouldn't have brought out the big guns this early in our relationship."

Jayme freaking loved that he'd come right out and said they were in a relationship. "I think you're good," she told him.

"Anyway, I thought I'd show you my house. That is...if you want to. I can take you back to Winnie's if you'd prefer."

Jayme sat up straighter in her seat. "I'd love to see

your place. You've talked about it enough that I'm insanely curious."

"It's nothing really special."

"Wrong," Jayme said immediately. "It's your home, and you love it. That makes it very special."

He gave her a small smile.

"Tell me more about it?" she asked.

"It's an older farmhouse on about three acres. It needed a lot of work when I bought it, but the first time I saw it, I fell in love. It has a wraparound porch that I pretty much had to re-build from scratch because the boards were all rotted. It's two stories, four bedrooms. I think I told you that I redid the kitchen and bathrooms, so they're completely modern, but I kept some of the older touches here and there. I used reclaimed wood where I could, and I have a gorgeous barn door separating my library from the great room. I did my best to make it more open concept, but since it's an older house, that was harder because there were a lot of the support beams I couldn't knock out." He paused and gave her a sheepish look. "Too much?"

"No, keep going," Jayme encouraged, loving his enthusiasm for his home.

"I wanted a basement—because this is Texas and tornados do happen—but it wasn't possible, so I built a cellar."

"Like in *The Wizard of Oz*?" Jayme asked excitedly.

Rocket chuckled. "Yeah, I guess so."

"So cool!"

"Well, you probably wouldn't think it was cool if a tornado was bearing down and you had to get in it," Rocket said dryly.

"I'd probably love it even more," Jayme mused.

"I'm still working on the landscaping. I've tried to minimize the grasses and trees that need a lot of water, because that's not environmentally responsible, so there's a lot of gravel and hardy shrubs, but I do have a section of the yard with the original trees still on it. They throw a lot of shade, and I've put up a hammock. One of my favorite things to do is simply to lie in it and take in my surroundings."

Jayme closed her eyes. She could totally picture Rocket lying in a hammock and swaying back and forth in the breeze.

More importantly, she could picture them lying there together.

"What was that thought?" Rocket asked.

The man was damn perceptive. "I was just wondering if we'd both fit in that hammock," Jayme said, trying to get over her shyness. There was something about this man that gave her the confidence to say what she was thinking.

"We will," Rocket said.

They shared a look so intimate, goose bumps broke out on Jayme's arms. She had to change the subject, otherwise she'd do something embarrassing... like reach for the button on his jeans and go down on him right there in the truck.

"Rocket's an unusual name," she blurted. "Is it a nickname?"

For a second, she didn't think he was going to let her change the subject. The heat in his eyes was almost scorching—and Jayme couldn't wait to get burned.

But as if he knew how on the edge she was, Rocket went with the change in subject. "It's my real name, not a nickname. I can show you my birth certificate if you want."

"I believe you," Jayme said. "No proof necessary."

"My mom wanted something unique for me, wanted to be different than her friends, who were naming their kids John, Rob, and Samuel. Of course, she didn't stop to think about how badly I'd get made fun of with a name like Rocket, but luckily I hit puberty pretty early and people didn't really want to mess with someone as big as me. I guess she chose Rocket because in her mind, it brought forth images of someone going somewhere. Being strong and aiming high." He shrugged a little self-deprecatingly.

"Being a mechanic wasn't exactly what she thought I'd end up doing though."

Jayme squeezed the hand she was still holding. "She doesn't approve of your profession?"

"It's not that she doesn't approve," Rocket said. "I mean, she was happy I went into the Navy, but I think she was hoping I'd be a literal rocket scientist or astronaut or something more prestigious. She loves me, we just aren't close."

"I think what you do is amazing. Sure, rockets are impressive, but someone has to design it. Someone has to keep it running. Someone has to fill it with fuel and make sure provisions are all loaded up so the astronauts are kept safe. Not to mention the people who stay on the ground and monitor the technology as that rocket is flying toward space. I think people are too impressed by those at the top, when they should be worshiping the little guys, the people who keep our economy going. The fast food workers, the people who work at gas stations, those at the big convenience stores and markets who work long hours stocking the shelves. Us little people are the ones who *really* keep the world going, not the head honchos at the top of the pile."

Jayme was a little embarrassed when she got done with her impassioned speech, but she couldn't stand to see Rocket feel any doubt about himself or what he did for a living.

Rocket divided his attention between her and the road for a long moment before bringing her hand up to his mouth and kissing the palm. His ever-present five o'clock shadow was scratchy against her hand.

"Besides," she said, her tone lighter, "I'm thankful that you're good at engines, because I'm hopeless when it comes to anything mechanical. I can change a tire, if I have to, but anything else with a car and I'm totally out of my depth."

"You've got me to change your tires now," Rocket said with no hesitation whatsoever.

"Awesome," Jayme said softly. She loved the thought that he'd be around if and when she ever had car trouble. The one time she'd broken down on Interstate 5 in Seattle had been extremely stressful. She'd had to wait almost two hours for the car service to show up and she'd been scared one of the cars whizzing by was going to hit her the entire time.

"This is my driveway," Rocket said as he pulled off the main road.

Jayme looked forward—and inhaled sharply when she saw Rocket's house.

It was gorgeous. And if she was in the market to buy a house, it was exactly what she'd want for herself. The wraparound porch made her want to pull up a rocking chair and hang out. Each window had adorable shutters and everything about the property was welcoming and peaceful.

"Oh, man, Rocket, I love it!"

"Good," he said as he drove around to the side of the house, pushing a button on the garage door remote. He pulled his truck into the bay and said, "I've got a large outbuilding on the other side where I restore vehicles and do the construction work for the house. The cellar is out back, I'll show both to you later, if you want."

"I want," Jayme said with a smile.

They both climbed out of the truck, and he held open the door to the house for her. "I'm not a good cook by any stretch, which you already know, but I do grill a good steak, or chicken if you prefer. That's... if you want to stay for dinner."

"I'd love to stay," Jayme told him. She turned around to face him before entering the house. She was a step above him and he was *still* taller than her. Feeling brave, Jayme wrapped her arms around his neck and rested her head on his chest. She could feel his heart beating under her cheek. "Thank you for an amazing date, Rocket," she told him. "But we could've sat in your truck in a Walmart parking lot and it still would've been awesome. I just like spending time with you. I know you're really busy, and I appreciate you spending your day off with me."

"Wasn't a hard choice," Rocket replied as his arms closed around her.

"I know you probably had stuff to get done."

"Nope. Nothing important," he countered.

They stayed like that for a long moment before Jayme pulled back. She didn't let go of him though. Instead, she looked up at him briefly before rising up on her tiptoes.

She pressed her lips to his and closed her eyes.

If she was afraid she was being too bold or overstepping, her fears were immediately put to rest when Rocket groaned and pulled her closer. He took over the kiss, tilting his head and licking her bottom lip, as if asking permission to enter. Jayme immediately granted him access, tightening her grip on him as he lifted her off her feet and entered his house. He towered over her, but it made her feel protected and cherished instead of overwhelmed.

Rocket pushed her back against the wall just inside the house and they kissed as if this was going to be the first and only kiss they'd ever share. It turned carnal quickly, which only made Jayme want him more. Their tongues intertwined and played, learning what each other liked. But throughout it all, Rocket didn't take advantage; his hands stayed locked around her body and didn't roam. Jayme desperately wanted to feel the calluses on his palms against her sensitive skin, but was enjoying their first kiss too much to want any distractions right that second.

When he finally pulled back, they were both breathing hard. Jayme saw his gaze flick to her chest and knew she should probably be embarrassed, because he had to see how hard her nipples were. But nothing about this felt awkward.

"I like your house," she whispered.

He grinned. "You haven't even seen it."

"Doesn't matter. I know it's perfect."

"You okay?" he asked, his brows furrowing a bit. "I don't want you to feel any pressure here. You're safe."

"I know I am," Jayme told him. Was two weeks enough to fall head over heels in love with someone? She had no idea, but had a feeling she was already a goner.

He lifted a hand and brushed his thumb over her lips. They felt a bit swollen, and she couldn't help but smile and flick her tongue out to lick over his skin.

"Fuck," Rocket muttered. "You're gonna be the death of me."

"But what a way to go," she sassed back.

"True. Come on. Let me show you my house."

Jayme nodded, ignoring the pang of disappointment when his arms dropped from around her and he stepped away. But he only went as far as the garage door they'd just entered through. After shutting it, he took her hand in his once more and held on firmly as he led her further into his beautiful home.

CHAPTER FIVE

Rocket let out a small breath of air and stilled when Jayme shifted against him. She was fast asleep, and had been for at least an hour. After dinner, when she'd insisted on helping by whipping up some home-made rolls—and chocolate chip cookies for dessert—they'd sat on his couch and he'd turned on the television. He had no idea what was on, as his complete attention was devoted to the woman in his arms. She'd snuggled against him, resting her head on his shoulder, and promptly fell asleep.

Rocket couldn't help but grin at remembering her reaction to his kitchen. Her eyes had gotten wide and she'd been speechless for a full minute. He'd told her that he'd gone all out with the kitchen and bath-rooms, but apparently she hadn't quite realized what that meant.

He had a restaurant-grade forty-eight-inch gas range with a huge double-sided refrigerator. Marble countertops and every kitchen gadget known to man. He'd gone overboard, and he knew it—especially for a man who didn't cook—but he'd hoped at some point to find a woman who might love the space.

The bathrooms were just as opulent, with heated floors, Jacuzzi tubs, double sinks, rain shower heads, more marble countertops. He'd had every intention of spoiling the woman he loved, and the best way he knew how was to make his home a refuge for her.

By Jayme's reaction, he'd succeeded. She was impressed with his bathrooms, but it was clear she could *live* in his kitchen. She'd had a huge smile on her face the entire time she'd been cooking, and Rocket knew he'd never spent a nicer evening in his house than this one.

She'd called Winnie and let her know where she was, and that she'd be home late. Winnie had, of course, told her to enjoy herself and not to worry about her—and that if she wanted to spend the night, it was perfectly all right with her. Jayme had blushed, and it had been all Rocket could do not to pull her into his arms and kiss the hell out of her once more.

She'd surprised him earlier with the kiss, but he hadn't hesitated to reciprocate. He'd been right; she fit against him perfectly. And no matter how badly he'd wanted to cup her lush ass and press her tight to his impossibly hard erection, he'd kept his hands in safe territory.

And now she was plastered to him and all he could smell was her flowery scent, torturing him. But he didn't dare move. Didn't want to disturb her.

He was still in awe that she was here at all. Yes, he'd wanted to find someone to spend the rest of his life with, someone he could love and cherish and who'd be devoted to him in return, but honestly, he didn't think that would happen.

And within a span of two weeks, here he was. Head over heels for the woman currently in his arms.

Rocket had thought falling in love would be comforting and easy. Instead, it was scary as hell. What if she didn't feel the same way about him? What if she got hurt or killed? How would he cope? If he could get her to reciprocate his feelings, what if she changed her mind down the line?

He was completely out of his element and terrified he'd do something wrong that would ruin his chance at happiness.

He must've tensed or otherwise moved, because Jayme shifted in his grip and opened her eyes as she tilted her head up to look at him.

She was so freaking beautiful. Rocket could stare

at her for hours and not get bored. Her dark blue eyes reminded him of the deep blue of the ocean.

"What time is it?" she asked huskily.

"Not too late," Rocket said softly.

"I didn't mean to fall asleep," she told him.

"It's okay. You had an eventful day."

She harrumphed, and Rocket grinned at how cute she was.

"Please. I've become so lazy now that I don't get up at the crack of dawn to get into the bakery. I feel as if all I do is sleep. When I first quit, I was happy to sleep in, to bake just for myself instead of for someone else. But I'm feeling the itch to get back to it. To make Warm Delights a reality."

"Then do it," Rocket said.

Jayme snorted. "It's not that easy."

"It's not," Rocket agreed. "But nothing worthwhile ever comes easy."

"Now you sound like Memaw."

Rocket couldn't help himself. He brought a hand up and ran it through her hair. He loved the way Jayme's head stayed on his shoulder, and how she closed her eyes as he stroked her.

"Rocket?" she asked without opening her eyes.

"Yeah?"

"I'm not tired anymore."

Rocket froze. Her words seemed to go straight to

his dick. He wanted to pick her up and carry her to his room and make love to her all night long, but he wasn't sure that was what she meant by her innocent words.

Her eyes opened again, and she moved, throwing a leg over his thighs and straddling him. She put her arms around his shoulders and looked him straight in the eyes as she clarified, "I've never felt this way about someone before. I don't know what it is about you, but I feel as if I'm right where I was meant to be. I've always despaired that my past relationships hadn't worked out. I thought there was something wrong with me. But being with you feels right. It's crazy, I know. And I'm talking too much and probably freaking you out. All I mean is that...I want you. Will you make love to me?"

Rocket's dick had stiffened the second her soft ass settled on his thighs, and it only got harder as she spoke. He swallowed, trying to clear his throat so he could speak. "Yes."

There was so much more he wanted to say. He wanted to tell her that he felt the same way. That from the second he saw her in Winnie's house, he felt as if he'd been hit with a two-by-four. That everything he'd done in his life seemed to narrow to that moment. But all he could get out was that one word.

Yes.

Scooting to the edge of the couch, Rocket moved his hands to Jayme's ass and held her to him as he stood. She didn't squeal in fright, didn't clutch him tighter. She simply smiled and hooked her ankles behind him.

"You're safe. I'm not going to drop you," Rocket told her, wanting to reassure her even though she didn't seem scared that he was carrying her.

"I know. For some reason, I always feel safe with you."

She couldn't know how much her words meant to him. For most of his life, he was the man who earned subtle side-eye glances from everyone. Not sure if they could trust him. Because of his size, people were always giving him a wide berth and crossing the street so they didn't have to walk past him. Her trust meant everything,

He stared into her eyes as he carried her up his stairs toward his bedroom. Rocket knew he should probably slow things down between them. They'd only been on a handful of dates, even if they *had* talked almost every day since they'd met. He didn't want her to regret sleeping with him. But he couldn't say no to her. Anything she wanted, he'd bend over backward to give to her.

Once in his bedroom, Rocket held on to her waist and tapped her hip. She obliged and dropped her legs until she was standing in his embrace. The difference in their sizes hit home once more, and Rocket knew he'd have to go slow so he didn't hurt her. The thought of how small and tight she'd be when he got inside her made his cock harden even further.

"I've got an extra toothbrush in the drawer, to the right of the sink I've been using," he told her.

"Thanks," she said gratefully. She stepped away from him, and for a second, Rocket panicked. He didn't want to let her go. What if she changed her mind? What if she wanted to go home?

As if she knew how anxious he was, Jayme placed her hand on his cheek and said softly, "I won't take long. Thanks for giving me the opportunity to freshen up."

Rocket nodded and watched as she padded over to his over-the-top bathroom. She shot him a small smile before closing the door behind her.

Running a hand through his short hair, Rocket took a deep breath. He was forty years old, for God's sake. He needed to get his shit together. But tonight felt different from every other time he'd been with a woman. More important. All-encompassing.

Walking quickly out of the room, he headed for the guest bathroom in the hallway. He brushed his teeth and washed his face before stripping his shirt over his head. Dropping it on the floor and not giving the material a second thought, he went back into his bedroom.

Then he hesitated. Should he take his pants off? Get into bed under the covers?

He felt awkward and unsure about everything. He didn't want to look too eager, but hell, he *was* eager.

He went over to the small table next to the bed and got out the box of condoms he'd bought that week. He hadn't assumed he and Jayme would do anything, but just in case, he'd wanted to be prepared. He opened the box and put one of the condoms within easy reach of the bed. Then he sat nervously on the edge of his mattress and waited for Jayme to reappear. His heart felt as if it was beating out of his chest...and he couldn't wait to make Jayme his.

Surprisingly, Jayme wasn't nervous. Okay, she was a *little* nervous, but she was more excited. When she'd woken up in his arms, she knew there was nowhere else she wanted to be. Around Rocket, she felt cherished. It was a heady feeling, and she couldn't stop herself from asking him to make love to her.

She'd never slept with a man after only a few dates, but everything within her was screaming that

Rocket was *it* for her. It was insane, but for once in her life, Jayme was going after what she wanted.

She appreciated him giving her the chance to freshen up. She brushed her teeth and used the restroom, then contemplated what to do next. Did she take off all her clothes and walk into his room butt naked? Did she wear a towel? Leave everything on?

Shoot. She wanted to be sexy and confident, but she'd never been completely comfortable in her own skin. She liked sampling her own wares a bit too much.

But this was Rocket. She'd seen him eyeballing her ass and boobs more than once. She didn't think he'd be turned off when he saw her naked, but she wasn't sure she could waltz out into his room without a stitch of clothing on either.

Deciding to compromise, Jayme took off her jeans, socks, underwear, and bra. She left on her shirt. It didn't hide much, but it went down to the top of her thighs, so her most important bits were covered. Scrunching her nose as she inspected herself in the floor-to-ceiling mirror behind the door, she took a deep breath. She was who she was, and if Rocket didn't like the way she looked, it was better to know sooner rather than later.

She opened the door and hesitantly stepped into the master bedroom.

Her eyes immediately went to Rocket, who was sitting on the edge of his bed. He'd taken his shirt off and was wearing only his jeans.

Hoping she looked more confident than she felt, Jayme took a step toward him. His eyes came up from the floor he'd been studying and met hers. Then he took her in, and his breath caught.

And just like that, Jayme felt her confidence return.

"Holy shit," he breathed as she neared. "You're so beautiful."

Jayme had a million responses to that. Her thighs were too big and rubbed together when she walked. She couldn't get rid of the belly pooch she'd had her entire life. Her hair was too thick; she always seemed to break out when she was super stressed; her toes were too short and stubby.

But instead, she lifted her chin and said, "Thank you. You're pretty amazing yourself."

Just as she reached him, Rocket went to his knees in front of her. Even kneeling, he was level with her chest. He really was tall. His hands hovered at her hips, but he didn't touch her.

"May I?" he asked, glancing at her face.

"Please."

Then his large hands were on her. At first, he simply rested them on her T-shirt at her hips...then they slowly inched down until he was touching the bare skin of her thighs. His gaze was fixed on her body—and he froze when he slowly pushed her shirt up far enough to realize she wasn't wearing panties.

His head jerked up, and Jayme could see the lust and longing in his eyes. "You're bare under here?" he asked.

It was a silly question, because it was obvious he'd already seen she was naked under her shirt, but she nodded anyway. "It seemed silly to wear them when they'd just be coming off anyway."

"Holy shit," Rocket said under his breath. Then he lifted her shirt above her waist and simply stared.

He did it for so long, Jayme began to fidget. "Rocket?"

"Sorry," he said, without looking away from her sex. "Trying to get control here. You're perfect."

She wasn't. Jayme knew that. But hearing the reverence in his words made her feel pretty for the first time in ages. She'd taken extra care with her grooming that week, making sure her pubic hair was trimmed neatly and her legs were smooth.

Rocket stood, towering over her once more. He took her shirt in his hands and lifted it up and over her head until she was standing in front of him completely naked.

He immediately began to unbutton his own pants, shoving them and his boxers down his legs before kicking them to the side.

Then he blew her mind by reaching out and pulling her into his arms.

They were skin to skin. Jayme could feel her breasts pressing against his rock-hard body, his erection pulsing hot and hard against her stomach. It was an intensely intimate moment, and he seemed content to simply hold her.

A few minutes later, Rocket pulled back. His gaze flicked to her hard nipples, still brushing against the hair on his chest, before he looked into her eyes. "Thank you," he said quietly.

"For what?" Jayme asked.

"For trusting me with you," he said simply. Then he sat on the bed and scooted backward.

His words settled into her heart, and Jayme swallowed hard to keep her emotions from overwhelming her. She followed him onto the bed and settled onto her side next to him. He immediately reached for her and lowered his head.

No words passed between them for the longest time as they kissed. Rocket's hands explored her body, touching, caressing, learning what kind of touch tickled and what made her moan. Jayme's hands were busy as well, loving the contrast between their bodies. Where she was soft, he was hard. Where she was smooth, he was rough.

When her fingers brushed over his pulsing cock, he made a strangled noise in his throat and crawled down her body.

"Rocket," she complained.

"If you touch me, I'm gonna explode," he admitted. "I want to make you feel good first."

"I do," she reassured him.

"Then I want to make you feel better," he returned, before lowering his head between her legs.

Jayme gasped and opened her legs even wider. She'd never understood what the fuss was about oral sex. In the past, she'd much preferred to use her own hand to help herself get off with a man, but all she could do at the moment was clutch the sheet below her and hang on for the ride.

Rocket used his mouth, his nose, his fingers, his teeth...he was one hundred percent focused on doing whatever he could to get her off. And it wasn't long before Jayme felt the telltale signs of an impending orgasm.

"Yeah, right there!" she begged as he began to lick her clit. She felt his finger gently fucking her, and she groaned. Her legs began to shake, and she grabbed ahold of Rocket's head as she hurtled over the edge of one of the most powerful orgasms she'd ever had in her life.

At the point when she usually backed off while pleasuring herself, Rocket intensified the attention on her clit.

"Rocket...enough..."

He merely grunted and added a second finger inside her pulsing sheath, flicking his tongue against her sensitive nub faster.

Jayme let out a small scream as her orgasm continued. She saw stars behind her eyes and all she could do was hold on and pray Rocket caught her when she fell.

She didn't know how much time had passed, but eventually she realized that Rocket was nuzzling her inner thigh. His fingers were still deep inside her body, and in the past, she would've felt embarrassed at how wet she was and how close his face was to her pussy. But amazingly, she wasn't now.

"Holy crap," she muttered. "Rocket?"

"Yeah?"

"Please fuck me."

He moved faster than she expected. His fingers pulled out of her protesting body and she watched as he smoothed on the condom he'd left by the bed.

She'd been right before, he *was* a big man. But Jayme wasn't nervous. Rocket would never hurt her.

The mushroom head of his cock pressed against her soaking-wet folds, and Jayme widened her legs as far as she could. Rocket groaned as he eased just his tip into her.

"Fuck, Jayme. You're so tight. I don't want to hurt you."

"You won't," she reassured him. Jayme kept her eyes on his cock, looking down her body as he ever so slowly pushed inside her.

He stopped when he was halfway in and threw his head back. His jaw was clenched and he looked like he was in pain.

Maybe because of how intense her orgasm had been, and how wet she still was, Jayme wasn't feeling any pain at all. Reaching over, she grabbed a pillow from beside her and lifted her ass just enough to shove the pillow underneath.

Rocket's eyes opened and he met her gaze for a split second...before his gaze lowered.

"That's so damn hot," he whispered.

And it was. Lifting her ass improved the angle of his entry, and he slid in the rest of the way. As their pubic hair meshed together Jayme sighed. She linked her ankles behind his ass and grabbed hold of his biceps.

"Move," she begged.

"I don't think I can. Not without coming," Rocket admitted.

Jayme chuckled. "I have faith in you," she told him.

Slowly, Rocket began to move his hips. He drew back then gently reentered her. Over and over, as if savoring the feel of her slick body around him. It felt nice, but Jayme wanted more. She wanted to see Rocket lose control. Wanted him to feel as good as he'd made her feel earlier.

"Harder, Rocket," she cajoled. "I'm not going to break."

"I'm a lot bigger than you," he said as he held on to his iron control.

"You are. And I love feeling you deep inside me. But I need *more*."

At that, his eyes met hers once more. And that was all it took.

"I'll always give you what you need," he said, and this time, instead of easing back into her, he slammed his hips forward.

They both moaned.

"Yessss," she hissed.

He did it again. And again. Until Jayme was once more awash in pleasure. The sound of his hips smacking against her flesh was loud in the room, seeming to echo around them, enhancing the pleasure.

Jayme stared up at Rocket in fascination. His upper chest was red and blotchy from his efforts, and he was panting as he took his pleasure. The muscles in his biceps rippled as he held himself up, not wanting to squish her as he fucked her hard.

Each thrust inside her pushed Jayme closer to orgasm. She'd never been one to be able to get off during actual intercourse, but because of Rocket's size, and how sexy he made her feel, she was on the verge once again.

Moving one hand between them, she couldn't resist caressing Rocket's cock as he pulled out of her body. He was slick with her excitement, and she used that to lubricate her clit as she flicked it.

"Damn," Rocket said. "Yes, get yourself off. I want to feel your tight pussy strangle my cock. Faster, Jayme. I'm close…"

His words spurred her to move her fingers faster, desperate to give him what he wanted. It didn't take long. Between his thrusts, his dirty talk, and the way his eyes bored into hers, Jayme was coming.

"Ah, shit, that is so fucking good!" Rocket said just as he began thrusting into her even harder than before. The entire bed jolted each time he pushed inside her, and Jayme knew her boobs were bouncing up and down with the motion.

She also knew the second Rocket lost it. One hand went under her ass and he pulled her in tight as he pushed into her one last time, holding himself as far inside her as he could get and throwing his head back. The veins in his neck stood out as he grunted his satisfaction.

Jayme dug her fingernails into his biceps and watched as he experienced the high only an orgasm could provide. It was over way too quickly for her liking, before his body slowly relaxed. He fell to the side, then onto his back, still clutching her ass. Jayme ended up straddling his lap, and she sat up, staring down at him.

His arms flopped out to his sides and his chest heaved up and down as he tried to catch his breath. "Holy shit, woman. You killed me," he quipped.

Jayme giggled and felt his cock twitch inside her. She raised an eyebrow.

He grinned. "Well, I'm not quite ready to go another round, but give me five minutes."

She wouldn't be surprised if that was true.

One of his hands came up and he lightly traced her nipple with his forefinger. It immediately hardened at his touch. His gaze met hers briefly, before he wrapped his arms around her and turned her onto her back. His cock slipped out of her, and Jayme moaned.

"I know. I need to take care of the condom. I'll be right back. Don't move."

Rocket eased out of the bed, but before he headed for the bathroom, he pulled the sheet and comforter up and over her body.

Jayme watched as he walked completely unself-consciously to the bathroom. He was back within a minute, climbing under the covers and taking her into his arms as if he'd done it every day for the last twenty years.

Jayme snuggled into him, feeling completely at ease. His fingers lightly traced her shoulder as they lay there, simply enjoying the feel of each other.

"Rocket?"

"Hmmm?"

"Thank you," Jayme told him quietly.

He didn't ask for what. Didn't tell her she didn't need to thank him. He simply said, "You're welcome."

CHAPTER SIX

Rocket couldn't remember a time before Jayme was in his life. Well, he could, but he didn't want to. He was as busy as ever with work, but the difference was, now when he came home, more often than not Jayme was at his house. She made dinner for them every night, and his house was always filled with the delicious scent of the delicacies she baked each day.

Winnie had hooked her up with a real estate agent, and she was close to signing the paperwork for the perfect space that would make Warm Delights a reality and Rocket couldn't be happier for her. He knew there was a lot of hard work ahead, and it would mean less time for her to spend with him, but it would be worth it to see her blossom.

Two months had passed since they'd first gotten together...and Rocket had just bought an engagement ring for her a couple days ago. She was the woman he wanted to spend the rest of his life with; he was just waiting for the perfect time to ask.

Even though she was spending every night with him at his house, she still visited her grandmother every day, checking on her and making sure she had everything she needed and wasn't lonely. Now it was Saturday, and they were spending it with Winnie at her house. She needed some yard work done, and Rocket had gladly volunteered. When her neighbors had seen him outside in the yard, they'd come over as well.

Kane Temple—known as Brain to his friend and teammates—was in the Army, and he frequently mowed Winnie's yard. His girlfriend, Aspen, came over when she saw Jayme and Winnie sitting on the porch. The three women had laughed and talked as he and Brain hauled away fallen limbs from a recent storm and tidied up Winnie's yard.

When they were done, they joined the women. Jayme had made some banana bread for her grand-mother, and Winnie graciously shared it with all of them as they relaxed on her porch.

"How's the new job going?" Winnie asked Aspen.

"It's good. Really good," she told her.

Winnie turned to her granddaughter and Rocket. "Aspen was in the Army. She was a combat medic. She got out and now she works for an ambulance company."

Rocket was impressed. "Combat medic, huh?" he asked.

But it was her boyfriend who responded. "Attached to a Ranger team," he informed them.

Rocket whistled low.

"What? What am I missing?" Jayme asked, looking confused.

"They're responsible for providing medical treatment for soldiers wounded on the battlefield," Rocket explained. "Army Rangers are some of the best-trained soldiers in the world. They're an elite force that conducts special military missions on short notice. To be attached to one of their units, a combat medic practically needs to be a Ranger him or herself."

Rocket noticed Brain smirking, but the other man didn't say anything.

"I didn't think women were allowed in combat?" Jayme asked.

"In 2013, the ban was lifted on women serving in combat, in 2015 the first woman graduated from Ranger school. Then in 2016, all combat jobs opened to women. It's been an uphill battle, pun intended, but ever so slowly, things are changing," Aspen said.

"Would it be rude for me to ask why you got out?"

Jayme asked. "I mean, you can ignore that question if you want. I'm just curious."

The other woman shrugged. "When I joined the Army, I had grand hopes that I'd be able to save the world. That I could make a difference. But not everyone is ready to embrace the fact that women can be just as effective on the battlefield as men."

"What she's *not* saying is that the men on the team she was attached to were assholes," Brain clarified. "She's an amazing paramedic, and the Army lost a hell of a medic when she quit. But their loss is Killeen's gain. She saved my life not too long ago."

The look of love and respect Brain shot his girlfriend was easy to read.

"Really?" Jayme asked.

Aspen shook her head. "I didn't do anything that anyone else wouldn't've have done," she protested.

"Wrong." Brain looked back at his audience. "It wasn't too long ago, during that tropical storm that made Houston flood so badly. We were sent down to the city to help out. I was...er...wounded, and ended up floating facedown in the floodwater. Aspen jumped out of the boat and dragged me to safety, giving me rescue breaths until I started breathing on my own. Then when we were separated from the other rescuers, she sat with me all night on a doorstep. If it hadn't been for her, I would've been a goner for sure."

"Holy crap!" Jayme said.

Rocket eyed the couple. He was astute enough to realize a lot of the details of whatever had happened were being left out, but the love between Brain and his girlfriend was as clear as day.

"You did something boneheaded after that though, didn't you?" Winnie berated.

Brain's brow furrowed. "Yeah."

"Memaw!" Jayme scolded.

"What?" Winnie asked.

"That wasn't polite."

The older woman scoffed. "I'm too old to worry about hurting someone's feelings. Everyone makes mistakes, and it's obvious they've gotten over it."

Rocket couldn't argue with that. The couple was obviously head over heels in love. Brain couldn't go more than a minute without turning his head to check on his girlfriend while they'd been working, and the pride in his tone now was obvious.

"Still. It was rude," Jayme insisted.

"I might be old, but I'm not an idiot," Winnie retorted. "What do I have to do all day but stare out the window and observe my neighborhood? There was a week or so when Aspen didn't visit Kane. Everyone else came to visit him, but not her."

"Right... So, after I got hurt, I pushed Aspen away. Thought she was better off without me," Brain said.

"Then you got your head out of your butt and realized you were being stupid," Winnie added.

Both Aspen and Brain chuckled. "Yes, ma'am," Brain said.

"Good. Because I like her," Winnie said with a smile. "I could have obnoxious neighbors who throw parties and leave their trash can at the curb for days after the truck comes, but you two don't do that."

"Nope," Aspen said with a smile. "And if you ever need anything, we're right next door and can come over at a moment's notice."

The other woman sent a meaningful glance toward Jayme.

"Which we're very thankful for," Jayme said gratefully.

"I'm not dying yet," Winnie griped. "I don't need anyone hovering over me, waiting for me to kick the bucket."

Jayme patted her hand. "No one said anything about hovering," she said, trying to smooth over the situation.

"What do you do?" Brain asked Jayme, effectively moving the subject away from Winnie's health.

"Right now, nothing. But I'm working on buying a

piece of property and opening my own business. A bakery."

Rocket thought it was comical how Aspen's eyes widened in excitement.

"Really?" she asked.

"Yeah."

"That's awesome! I'm not a bad cook, but I'm a horrible baker. I think the world needs more cupcakes."

The two women smiled at each other.

"Tell her the name," Winnie told her granddaughter.

Jayme rolled her eyes, but complied. "I'm planning on calling it Warm Delights."

"Ooooh, I love it!" Aspen exclaimed.

"Thanks. Me too. I moved here to Texas when the opportunity to own my own bakery in Seattle fell through. I wasn't sure what I was going to do for work, but Rocket kind of helped me see that just because things didn't go the way I'd wanted in Seattle, that didn't mean I couldn't open a bakery here."

"Damn straight," Winnie said.

"Are you going to make birthday cakes and stuff for people or will you stick with just selling cookies and breads and stuff like that?" Aspen asked.

Rocket hadn't planned on interjecting himself into the conversation about Jayme's bakery, but he couldn't help himself. "She's gonna take specialty orders, but only a specific number a day...say, around five or so. So people will have to think ahead and move fast if they want to get on her list."

Jayme turned to gape at him in surprise, but Aspen and Brain nodded.

"Smart. Establish a situation where people can't just pop in and order something on the fly. It'll create a demand for your services, even become something special that people will hopefully bend over backward for," Brain said with a smile.

"Exactly," Rocket told him.

Conversation turned to Winnie's latest outing, when she and her friends went to a bar instead of heading to the senior center for bingo, and how much fun they'd had.

Glancing over at Jayme, who'd become subdued, Rocket could tell she was annoyed. He knew he'd overstepped, but he hadn't meant to upset her.

Aspen and Brain stayed to chat for another twenty minutes or so, but eventually they said they needed to get going. After several promises to stay in touch, they wandered back over to their house.

"We should probably get going too," Rocket said. He didn't have any plans for the night, but he had a feeling if he didn't clear the air with Jayme, he'd be sleeping alone—which wasn't something he ever wanted to do again.

He was addicted to Jayme. Loved falling asleep with her in his arms and loved waking up with her next to him, as well. He even liked that, despite her claim to the contrary, she wasn't a morning person... at least not until she'd had two cups of coffee. He loved everything about her, and having her in his house was a dream come true.

He could tell Jayme wanted to argue. Wanted to stay at her grandmother's house longer, but he needed to explain why he'd said what he had. He'd been thinking about her bakery for weeks now, and they'd even had several discussions about the business, and he wanted her to succeed more than he wanted just about anything in his life.

Without a word, Jayme headed into the house to grab her purse.

"You done stepped in it now," Winnie told him. But she was grinning as she said it.

"I know," Rocket admitted.

"For the record, I think what you said is a good idea. But my granddaughter's always been a bit stubborn. Once she gets something in her head, she just goes for it. Which isn't a bad thing, mind you, but she forgets to look up and assess every now and then."

Rocket nodded. He'd noticed that about Jayme,

and it was one of a hundred things he loved about her. The passion she had for life was exciting and seemed to permeate everyone around her. He'd gladly protect her from anyone who wanted to sabotage that excitement or take advantage of her. He could be the bad guy without any issue, but she needed to know that he was always, one hundred percent, on *her* side.

"I appreciate your support," Rocket told Winnie.

"You're good for her," the older woman said. "I can spot a con man a mile away, and you, Rocket Long, are anything but. I was lucky enough to be with my Steve for over fifty years. I always wanted that for my Jayme, and was beginning to despair of her finding her soul mate. But the second you offered to help me in that grocery store, I knew you would be good for her."

Winnie's words meant a lot to Rocket, even if he thought she was a little crazy. "Thanks," he said diplomatically.

Winnie chuckled. "You don't believe me, and that's okay. I'm just a senile old lady who you're humoring, and I don't care. But, I have to say, I'm not getting any younger, and I'd like to hold my great-grandchild at least once before I pass on to be with my Steve."

Rocket blinked in surprise. Years ago, he'd

thought about having children. About being a father. But as time passed, he'd pushed those desires to the back of his mind. Now, the image of Winnie holding a tiny baby flashed in his mind and wouldn't leave.

Then he pictured Jayme, round with their child... and instead of freaking him out, something settled deep inside his belly.

He wanted a family with Jayme.

Leaning forward, Rocket kissed Winnie's cheek and whispered, "I'm workin' on it."

"Good," she replied with a smile. "Oh, and you should know, I told Jayme that I want to walk her down the aisle, so don't go elopin' or nothin'."

"Noted," Rocket said with a chuckle.

"What's noted?" Jayme asked as she reappeared on the porch.

"That since you gave away my banana bread today, you need to make me a replacement loaf," Winnie said without missing a beat.

Jayme rolled her eyes, but smiled. "Of course, Memaw. You need help getting inside?"

"What am I, an invalid?" her grandmother asked. "Of course I don't need help! I'm gonna sit out here for a while longer. It's almost time for the neighbors across the way to get home, and they always come over to say hello. You know that."

"Right, sorry," Jayme said. Then she leaned over

and kissed her grandmother. "Call if you need anything."

"I will, but I won't," Winnie said.

"I can't believe I understood that," Jayme said with a small laugh. "Love you, Memaw."

"Love you too, child," Winnie responded. "Don't be too hard on him."

Jayme pressed her lips together and shook her head. "See you tomorrow."

Rocket wasn't surprised Jayme didn't rise to her grandmother's bait. She'd wait until she had him alone to lambaste him.

CHAPTER SEVEN

Jayme was able to keep her ire to herself all the way back to Rocket's house. It wasn't that she didn't want Rocket talking to Aspen and Brain about her bakery. It was more that it kind of sounded like he'd had all the ideas about her bakery. Yes, he had a business degree and had some really good ideas, but it wasn't as if she was an idiot. Jayme knew she was working herself up over Rocket's words, but she couldn't help but feel as if she had back in Seattle. That her ideas were brushed aside and not as important as a man's.

She even kept quiet when he politely asked if she wanted him to grill up some steaks or chicken for dinner.

But when Rocket asked if she wanted to talk now, or calm down a little before they talked, she lost it.

"Calm down?" she asked in amazement. "You didn't just say that to me."

Rocket crossed his arms over his chest, leaned a hip against his amazing marble countertop in his perfect kitchen in his perfect house, and had the gall to grin at her as if she was amusing as hell.

"Just because you're sleeping with me doesn't give you the right to take over my life."

Jayme knew she was being dramatic, but his comment to Memaw's neighbors had rubbed her the wrong way and she couldn't stop thinking about them.

"I know it doesn't," Rocket said calmly.

For some reason, instead of making her angrier, his non-reaction actually helped Jayme rein in her temper. She brushed past him and got a teabag down from the cabinet.

Rocket reached over and flicked the button on the tea kettle to heat the water. "Go sit, I'll get this ready for you," he told her.

Nodding, Jayme headed for the couch. She watched as Rocket prepared her tea, just like he did every night. There sure were so many considerate things he did for her on a daily basis.

She hadn't been sure if being around him all the time was going to work in the long run. She was so used to living on her own. But Rocket had made the transition seamless. She hadn't even consciously moved in with him, so much as she'd just kind of stayed after that first night. She enjoyed being with him, and even puttering around his house when he was at work just felt...right. She visited Memaw every day, but then came back here and made dinner for them both. And she baked—a lot. She enjoyed coming up with new recipes and concoctions for Rocket to try.

She also appreciated that he didn't always gush over every creation. There were certainly times when he'd suggested something wasn't quite right. That a cookie needed more chocolate or less nuts or something.

And she couldn't deny how *right* sleeping in his arms felt.

Jayme had never had a boyfriend she'd clicked with so quickly.

Which was why his making decisions for her bakery without discussing it with her first had bothered her so much. It wasn't as if what he'd told Memaw's neighbors was written in stone or anything; she knew she could do whatever she wanted with specialty orders. But Rocket just acting as if what he said was law really bothered her.

He headed over to the couch and held out a steaming cup of her favorite cinnamon-apple tea. Then, instead of sitting in the huge easy chair next to the couch, he sat next to her.

Right next to her. His thigh touched hers from knee to hip.

She frowned at him and scooted over, putting some space between them. But Rocket simply shifted with her, eliminating the space she'd gained.

"Rocket, I'm still annoyed with you. Can you scoot over?"

"No," he said without hesitation. "I know you're pissed, and I want to talk about it. I don't want to give you space because there's nowhere in the world I'd rather be than right by your side."

Okay, that was sweet...but Jayme was still annoyed. She blew out a breath and decided to just get it over with. "Fine. I'm still working out the details of my bakery. While I have a basic business plan that I worked on back in Seattle, I haven't decided about things like inventory, inventory options, or what I'm going to do about specialty orders. So why'd you tell Aspen and Kane that I'd only take a few orders a day?"

Rocket took a deep breath. "Right. I overstepped, I know that. But I did so from a good place."

Jayme waited, and when he didn't continue, she raised her eyebrows. "And?"

"The last two months, I've been happier than I can remember being in a very long time."

His words felt good, but they didn't explain why he'd made it seem as if he knew better than she did when it came to her business.

"Before you came into my life, I didn't have much to look forward to every day. I enjoy my job, I like my coworkers, I get a rush when I discover a problem with an engine and fix it. But every day was the same. I'd get up, work out, grab something for breakfast, go to work, then come home, eat takeout, and maybe tinker in my garage for a while before going to sleep. I occasionally went out with friends from work, but since most of them have families, those times were few and far between. When I met Winnie at the grocery store, she gave me something to do other than hang around my house being bored.

"Then, when I first saw you at Winnie's house, something clicked inside me. You were funny, and gorgeous, and I couldn't stop thinking about you from day one. Talking to you became the highlight of my days. I couldn't wait to get home from work so I could check my texts or call you. And all that sounds pathetic, and I know it, but it's the truth."

"I'm sure you had dates," Jayme said quietly.

Rocket's words were getting to her. She had no idea what his confession had to do with what had happened today, but it was almost impossible to stay mad at him when he was being so sweet.

Rocket shook his head. "Not really. Maybe I'm just picky in my old age, but I never felt a connection with anyone I met. Some were too desperate to be taken care of, others weren't interested in anything serious. Some just wanted sex, and a few were simply bitches who thought any man they dated should get down on his knees and thank his lucky stars they were with her. You weren't *any* of those things. You were shy, and slightly awkward, and nervous, and ambitious. You weren't looking for a husband...or even a date."

Jayme chuckled. "Wow, that doesn't make me sound very attractive."

He smiled at her. "It was. It *is*. Trust me. Anyway, now I get to wake up with you in my arms. See your smile. Hear your laugh. Savor your zest for life. I go to work in a good mood, and no matter what happens while I'm there, I know at the end of the day, I'm going to get to be with you. I walk into this house and it feels like a home for the first time since I first moved in. When I see you in the kitchen with an apron around your waist, I can't believe how lucky I am. And I don't mean just because you cook dinner and treats for me. It's because of *you*. You could tell me you're not making one more meal and I wouldn't care, as long as I still got to come home to you.

"And I love that you're working toward your goal of opening your own bakery. I'm so proud of you, my heart can barely stand it. Warm Delights is going to be a hit, I know it. How can it be anything else with your enthusiasm and excitement? And...when Aspen asked if you were going to take special orders, I had an immediate vision of the future. Of you getting up at four a.m....and not coming home until ten at night. Of you staying late every day because you had more cakes you had to bake for birthdays. Of one more batch of cookies you had to get done that someone ordered at the last minute for a retirement ceremony.

"I had an immediate flash of *jealousy*. It's stupid. I know. But the thought of you working day and night, of not getting to spend as much time with you...it hurt. I'm not being sexist; I know that I work all day, and I have no problem with you doing the same. But I want evenings to be *ours*. I don't know what you're thinking about as far as store hours go, but I hate the thought of you working fourteen hours a day. I just thought if you limited the special orders, you'd be able to leave the store to your manager and employees and come home at a reasonable hour.

"Creating scarcity really *is* a good marketing strategy. If customers know that they can't simply call in an order whenever they feel like it, the value of what you do will hopefully rise. But yeah...I was out of line with my assumptions, and of course you can do whatever you want with Warm Delights. But I said what I said because I love you and want to spend as much time with you as possible."

Jayme's irritation faded away with every word out of Rocket's mouth. How could she be upset that her boyfriend wanted to spend time with her? Yes, he *had* been out of line by telling Memaw's neighbors how she was going to run her business. But he'd said it out of an emotional need...and, she had to admit, an acute business acumen as well.

Then his last words registered. "You love me?"

"More than I'd ever thought I could love anyone," Rocket replied.

And just like that, Jayme was glad he hadn't let her put any space between them. She put her tea down on the coffee table in front of her and practically threw herself at Rocket. He caught her—of course he did—and held her tightly against him.

"I love you too," she said into his neck.

She felt him tighten his arms around her before his lips nuzzled her ear. "Enough to forgive me for speaking out of turn?"

Jayme pulled back so she could look into his eyes.

"Of course. There's nothing to forgive. Although I would like to request that maybe before you announce to others how I'm going to run my business, you maybe discuss it with me first?"

"Absolutely."

God, she loved this man. She should've known he wasn't trying to take over and make decisions about her bakery without her input. And she had to admit that it was probably a good marketing move to limit the number of specialty items she made each day. She knew she'd probably do just as he projected...stay at work until everything was done. "I'm not saying I want to make dinner every night for the rest of our lives, but for now, I like our routine. I like being here when you get home. I look forward to hearing your truck coming down the driveway. It isn't exactly a hardship cooking in your kitchen."

"Maybe you could teach me some basics. That way I can make something more than just grilled steak and chicken."

"You'd like that?" Jayme asked.

"If you were my teacher, I'd love it," Rocket said.

Immediately, easy recipes started flitting through her head. Teaching him to cook would be fun, she suspected. "Deal."

"But maybe not right this second," Rocket said,

lowering his head and licking the side of her neck before nipping her gently.

"No? You have something else in mind?" Jayme asked with a huge grin on her face.

"Maybe," Rocket said. "But if you're tired, or still irritated with me, we can pass."

"I'm not tired or irritated with you," Jayme said, spreading her legs as Rocket's hand made its way from her knee to her inner thigh.

Without warning, he stood, then bent to haul her over his shoulder.

Jayme shrieked with laughter and propped her hands on his ass as he carried her toward the stairs. "Don't drop me!" she exclaimed.

"Never," Rocket vowed.

An hour later, Jayme lay in bed feeling completely boneless. Rocket had outdone himself, showing her exactly how much he loved her. She'd come twice, and he'd made love to her in more positions than she could count. How he'd managed to last as long as he had before losing control and coming deep inside her body, she had no idea.

They'd stopped using condoms recently, and she was on the pill. She loved that he didn't have to pull out right after they made love. She wouldn't have pegged Rocket as a man who enjoyed cuddling, but he always gathered her close and held her against his fiercely beating heart after he came, nuzzling the sensitive skin of her neck as they both calmed down.

She was currently lying on his chest, his semi-soft cock still inside her body, enjoying the aftermath of their lovemaking, when her stomach growled loud in the silence of the room.

Rocket immediately began to chuckle, which made his cock slip out of her body. Jayme lifted her head and mock-scowled at him, which only made him laugh harder.

"Sorry, love, I'm not laughing at you," he said.

She enjoyed hearing him call her "love," but she wrinkled her nose at him. "Um, I beg to differ. You most certainly *are* laughing at me," Jayme countered.

"Okay, true. You're just too damn adorable. Stay here," he ordered as he lifted her as easily as always and began to slip out from under her.

"Where are you going?" she pouted, hating to end their cuddling time.

"To get dinner," Rocket said easily.

"I'm not sure I want a steak right about now," Jayme told him, completely serious, since it was about all he could make.

"No steak. Trust me. I want to get back to your beautiful naked body as soon as I can. I'll be right back."

Jayme watched as he strode toward the closet. In

the last two months, most of her clothes had migrated into his closet and drawers. She'd lived out of a suitcase until Rocket had pointed at three drawers and said, "I moved my shit around so you can unpack." And that was that.

He pulled on a pair of boxers and nothing else, then gave her a small chin lift before heading out of the bedroom door.

Falling back on the mattress with a sigh, Jayme stared up at the ceiling. It was almost scary how much she loved Rocket. Sure, he could be annoying at times, but she knew she wasn't exactly Miss Congeniality all the time either. She thought they'd done an amazing job of learning to live together after both of them being single for so long.

The ceiling fan above her head spun lazily, mesmerizing Jayme...and the next thing she knew, she was startled awake when Rocket returned. She had no idea how long she'd dozed.

Sitting up, she watched him approach the bed with a large plate. Propping pillows behind her and pulling the sheet up to cover her nakedness, she smiled as Rocket placed his burden on the covers and got settled next to her.

He leaned over and kissed her before gesturing to the plate. "I made one of those fancy hors d'oeuvre plates."

He'd cut up some cheese, sliced some summer sausage, included some grapes, cantaloupe, watermelon, and black olives, and placed Cheez-It crackers all around the outside of the plate. "It's a charcuterie board!" Jayme exclaimed, laughing.

Rocket shrugged. "If that's what you want to call it. I hope it's okay?"

Jayme immediately turned to him. "It's perfect. Thank you."

"Well, it's not worthy of Chef Jayme Caldwell, but I'll get better."

"You can't get better," she told him seriously. "You're already perfect."

"Far from it, but I'm going to do my best to try to never let you down."

"You won't," Jayme whispered.

"I will," Rocket countered. "But I'll apologize when I do and promise to try harder. Like I did today."

"I love you," Jayme told him.

"And I love you back." Rocket picked up the plate and balanced it on his lap, putting an arm around her waist and pulling her against him. "What would mademoiselle like to try first?"

Giggling, Jayme reached for a grape and popped it into her mouth. She didn't know what the future held for her and Rocket, but she hoped they'd always be as happy as they were right this moment. She never wanted to go to bed mad and was glad he'd insisted they talk as soon as they got home.

She needed this man in her life...and was so thankful Winnie had set them up.

CHAPTER EIGHT

Rocket leaned against the wall of the soon-to-be-opened Warm Delights and smiled as he watched Jayme point out things to the contractor she'd hired. The closing for her store had gone off without a hitch three weeks ago, and she'd be opening her bakery after Christmas. She'd been busy setting up vendors, advertising, and getting the store designed exactly how she wanted it.

He loved witnessing the enthusiasm Jayme had and mentally swore to do whatever it took to make sure he cultivated it. She'd interviewed a few people earlier that morning and told him she was almost ready to make a decision on who to hire. Rocket had been able to get off a bit early so he could take her out to dinner to celebrate all her hard work.

Thanksgiving had come and gone, and she'd been

working extremely hard lately and he wanted to give her some time to sit and relax. Rocket couldn't help but smile when he thought about the night she'd signed the paperwork for the store. She'd been over the moon excited, and he couldn't remember when he'd smiled or laughed more when making love.

Jayme was the woman he'd dreamed about in his lonelier days. When he'd thought about the kind of person he wanted to spend his life with, she was it. She didn't let things get her down, was always upbeat, fun to be around, sensual, and considerate. Rocket was damn lucky, and he knew it. He wanted to be her rock, the person she looked to when she was happy, sad, frightened. He wanted to be everything to her.

So he'd talked to his boss and managed to get the afternoon off so he could be here when Jayme met with her contractor. He'd done some work already, and they'd both been pleased with it, so now Jayme was discussing the second phase of her vision for the bakery.

She looked over and caught his eye and smiled at him. Rocket grinned back and waited for her to finish her overenthusiastic explanation of what she wanted where, and which paint colors she wanted the man to use.

Twenty minutes later, the contractor said he'd get some drawings made up for her to look at within a week. She shook his hand and walked toward Rocket as the man left. She walked into his personal space and lay her head on his chest.

He wrapped his arms around her and asked, "Happy?"

"Extremely," Jayme replied, but then, strangely, she pulled out of his arms and headed for the door.

Standing up straight, wondering what was wrong, Rocket watched as she merely locked the front door and came back toward him.

When she got close enough, Jayme grabbed his hand and started to tow him toward the back of the space, into the kitchen area. Frowning, Rocket asked, "You all right, love?"

"I'm great," she said perkily, stopping in front of the huge countertop she'd had installed. It was big enough for several people to roll dough at the same time. Someone could decorate a cake on one side, while someone else prepared cookies or cupcakes or whatever. It was gray marble, and Rocket couldn't help but be flattered it mirrored the counter in his own kitchen. Jayme had told him she loved his kitchen so much that she couldn't imagine anything better than copying the design here in her store.

She hopped up on the counter and crooked her finger at him. "Have I told you lately how much I appreciate you helping me get my bakery up and running?"

"Yup," Rocket told her. "And while we both trust your contractor, I'm not one hundred percent comfortable with you being here alone with him."

"Rocket, he's like sixty-five, I didn't think he was gonna jump me while I explained what I wanted for the public space of my store."

"Don't care," Rocket said. And he didn't. He didn't think the man would've done anything to hurt Jayme, but he also wasn't willing to take that chance. "Besides, I really just wanted to spend some time with you today. I feel as if we haven't had much lately."

"I know," Jayme said, as she pulled him toward her. She spread her legs apart and hooked her ankles together at the small of his back. "You've been working really hard too. Everything all right?"

"Yeah. A few units are getting ready to deploy after the holidays and we've been working overtime to make sure the choppers are all in tip-top shape for them."

"I'm proud of you," Jayme said, and Rocket felt his chest expand.

He liked making her proud. It felt good. "So? Did you have something in mind when you dragged me back here?"

She grinned. "Maybe," she said coyly.

Rocket *loved* when she got like this. He wanted her pretty much every minute of every day, but he did his best to rein in his libido so he didn't overwhelm her. She didn't usually make the first move when it came to sex, but when she did, their encounters were always over-the-top hot.

"Here?" he asked, wanting to make sure she felt comfortable. They'd made love here before, but that was right after she'd bought the building and there hadn't been anything inside other than cobwebs and a few bits of odd furniture.

"I want to think about you every time I'm in here. When I'm icing a cake, I want to think of your hands on me. When I'm rolling out the dough for home-made bread, I want to remember the look in your eyes when you orgasmed. So yeah, Rocket. Here."

"Fuck, I love you," he said reverently, then immediately grasped the hem of her blouse and drew it up and over her head.

Jayme laughed and leaned back on her hands, thrusting her chest forward. Rocket was thrilled with how, over the months they'd been together, she'd lost a lot of her shyness around him. He adored how she looked and made sure to tell her every day.

She unhooked her legs from around his waist and

spread them as far apart as she could before she lay back on the cold marble.

"Looks like there's a feast laid out just for me," Rocket quipped.

Jayme laughed and lifted her head. "Just for you. Only you," she told him.

Rocket quickly unbuttoned her jeans and opened the zipper. He ripped her jeans and underwear off her legs, and her laugh turned into a moan when his hands lifted her ass and his head dropped.

An hour and a half later, they were on the way home. Rocket couldn't remember being this happy and sated. The ring he'd bought a couple months ago was burning a hole in his pocket, so to speak. He'd wanted to ask her to marry him a hundred times since he'd bought it, but he also wanted to make his proposal a moment she'd always remember. And he hadn't been able to come up with anything that he thought was good enough.

He hated that slight insecurity, but he never wanted her to feel cheated about anything to do with their relationship. He wanted to give her a story she could pass on to their kids.

Kids. God, he wanted to see her beautiful blue

eyes on a daughter of their own. Their children would hopefully inherit her smile, her nose, her complexion. He already loved them more than he could ever say, and they hadn't even done more than talk about the fact they wanted kids...someday.

"Rocket?" she asked.

"Yeah, love?"

"Thank you for believing in me."

"Always," he told her fervently.

"I know the building cost a ton, and the money it's costing to renovate things and to make it fit my vision is over the top, but it means a lot to me that you haven't, not once, told me I'm being ridiculous. That maybe I should be more frugal until I know if the bakery is gonna be successful."

Rocket reached for her hand and held it tightly. "One, if you half-assed your business, people would notice and wouldn't take you as seriously. Two, you're not being ridiculous at all. It's your money, you've saved for a long time, and I'd be a douche if I started dictating what you can and can't spend it on. And three, there's no 'if' about it, Warm Delights is gonna be successful. Wanna know how I know?"

"How?" she asked, tears shining in her eyes.

"Because I've eaten your treats. And they're fucking phenomenal. Anyone who orders something from your shop is immediately going to become a repeat customer. I predict within six months of opening your doors, you're going to have every special order slot filled for months in advance. You're going to have to hire more help, and you'll even need to think about expanding."

The tears fell over her cheeks. "I don't know about all that, but your confidence in me means the world."

Rocket lifted his hand and carefully wiped away a tear from her cheek. "*You* mean the world to me," he said simply. "Now, quit cryin' or you'll give me a complex. I just made you come three times, and *I* came so hard I saw stars. I want to go home, get you a cup of tea, and talk about our schedule for the next few weeks. Brain and Aspen invited us to hang out with their crew and celebrate the holidays with them one weekend. Your parents have talked about coming down here to Texas to visit, and I should probably extend an invite to my folks as well. Then Winnie wants to have a party for her friends too. I'm sure you're going to want to bake something for all of our get-togethers, so we need to figure all that out."

By the time he'd finished talking, Rocket saw that Jayme had pulled herself together. He loved when she got all gooey and emotional, but he hated to see her cry. He knew talking about the upcoming holiday parties would pull her out of her head, and he smiled when she nodded and immediately reached for her phone. The next few weeks were going to be hectic, but he couldn't be happier.

He'd always spent the holidays alone, and now with Jayme in his life, he had more social activities planned than he ever could've imagined. But he wouldn't change one thing about his life. Especially if it meant not having Jayme by his side.

CHAPTER NINE

Jayme was blissfully happy. Warm Delights was ready to open on January second. It was December twenty-third, and she was at Memaw's house preparing a huge Christmas dinner. Over the last few weeks, she and Rocket had attended quite a few get-togethers. She'd baked cookies, cakes, bread, pastries, and pies. She'd even made a fruitcake at Memaw's request.

Her parents had flown in and spent a few days getting to know Rocket and catching up on their daughter's life. They'd ooh and aahed over her bakery and told her how proud they were of her. Even Rocket's mom and dad had visited. He wasn't as close with his family, but he'd said afterward it felt good to at least try to connect with them once again.

They'd hung out with Memaw's neighbors when they'd had a big party, and Jayme had really enjoyed getting to know all of Aspen and Kane's friends. The men were all buff and strong, and she appreciated seeing how loving they were with their women.

All-in-all, it had been a great month of December, but Jayme was ready to hunker down for a few days with just Rocket. They'd been on the go so much they hadn't had a lot of time to spend with just the two of them. After tonight's dinner, they'd both decided they would take until the twenty-seventh to do nothing but be with each other.

No work for either of them. No visiting Memaw (although Jayme would check on her via phone every day to make sure she was all right), and no thinking about all the work she still had to do to open Warm Delights on the second. It would be just them, enjoying each other's company and feeling loved.

But first, they were celebrating Christmas with Memaw.

Rocket had been called into work for an emergency repair on one of the helicopters and he'd apologized a hundred times before Jayme had finally shooed him out of the house. "The sooner you go, the sooner you'll be back," she'd told him.

"Thank you for understanding," he'd said.

"Of course. There will be times I'll probably need to head down to the bakery on my time off because of some catastrophe. Besides, as much as you've learned in the kitchen, you'll just be in my way. Go, and when you get back, there'll be a nice Christmas dinner waiting for you."

"Love you," Rocket had said as he leaned down and kissed her on the forehead.

"Love you too."

Now she and Memaw were happily talking about her new Jazzercise class she was taking down at the YMCA. It was for seniors, and they all sat in chairs as they be-bopped to music.

"I think you should come with me one day," Memaw said.

Jayme rolled her eyes. "I don't think so."

"It'll be fun."

Her grandmother's idea of fun and Jayme's were quite different. But to get her off her back, she said, "I'll think about it."

Memaw turned to her with her hands on her hips. "No, you won't. You're just saying that to shut me up."

Jayme couldn't help but laugh. "True. Is it working?"

"No," Memaw griped.

Jayme chuckled again. "Will you please hand me the milk?"

Memaw frowned. "Milk?"

"Yeah, the stuff that comes from cows? I decided to double this cookie recipe because I want to make sure you have enough to tide you over until I come by again."

"Lord, child, how many cookies do you think I'm gonna eat?" Memaw asked.

"I know you, Memaw," Jayme said. "You'll get bored, and you'll want to feed Aspen and Kane. Then you'll call one of your friends to meet up. You'll hand out cookies to your mail delivery person, and anyone else you might see. I just want to make sure you've got enough."

Her grandmother laughed. "Right, okay, I see your point. But seriously, I think I'll be okay for four days while you and Rocket are locked inside his house."

Jayme blushed but turned to glance at her grandmother. "Why are you trying to talk me out of doubling this batch of cookies?"

Memaw held up the empty half-gallon container of milk. "Because we're out of milk."

"Well, crap," Jayme said in dismay. She glanced at her watch. "The convenience store down the street is still open. I'll just run down there and grab another one."

"Why don't you just go knock on Kane's door?"

"Because I need more than just a cup or so," Jayme argued as she went to the sink to wash her hands. "The mashed potatoes could probably use another dash once they sit for a while, and Rocket might want a glass with his dinner. I won't take too long."

"Rocket should be back soon. You could text him and ask him to pick it up on his way," Memaw said.

"I don't want to bother him. It'll just take ten minutes or so," Jayme replied breezily. "Stir the gravy while I'm gone, and check the turkey. You shouldn't need to take the aluminum foil off yet, but just check on it."

"I know how to cook, missy," her grandmother said a little huffily. "Who do you think taught *you*?"

Jayme leaned down and kissed Winnie on the cheek. "You did. And okay, I'll be right back. Love you."

"Love you too," her grandmother said as Jayme grabbed the keys to the car Memaw still had but didn't drive much anymore.

Ten minutes later, Jayme wished she'd taken her grandmother's advice and had texted Rocket instead of dashing down to the store herself.

Rocket was glad the problem at work wasn't terribly difficult to solve. He was a little annoyed they'd bothered him at all, but he didn't say anything to the captain who'd greeted him at the shop when he'd arrived. He was grateful to have a job he loved, even if it meant it took him away from his girlfriend more than he liked.

He reminded himself that once Warm Delights opened, he and Jayme would have even less time to spend together, although she'd decided to close her doors at two in the afternoon every day. She'd open at five in the morning and use the late afternoons to prepare the special orders for the next day. She should be home by dinnertime most days, and at least they'd have every evening together.

That was the plan at least, but Rocket knew as her bakery got more successful, she'd probably need to revisit her hours. But she could always hire more staff to be at the store while she headed home. He'd just have to give her a damn good reason to want to come home every afternoon instead of working late.

Smiling as he pulled into Winnie's driveway, he knocked on her door before heading inside. The interior of the house smelled delicious and his stomach immediately began to rumble. He still hadn't gotten used to eating as well as he had since meeting Jayme.

She might claim that baking was her forte, but she was a hell of a good cook as well.

"Hey, Winnie," he said as he entered the kitchen and saw Jayme's grandmother standing by the stove.

"Hi, Rocket. Everything go okay at work?"

"Yup. Where's Jayme?"

"She decided I needed twenty-eight dozen cookies instead of just one, and we ran out of milk. So she ran down to the convenience store to buy some more."

"Why didn't she text me to pick it up on my way?" Rocket asked with a frown.

Winnie laughed. "That's what I told her to do, but she said it would just take a few minutes."

"Okay. I'll head down there to meet up with her," Rocket said.

"I'm sure she'll be right back," Winnie protested. She looked up at the clock hanging on the wall in the kitchen. "She just left a few minutes ago."

"If I pass her, I'll just turn around and follow her home," Rocket said. He didn't know why he felt the pressing need to go to the store. He'd missed her, but he always did while he was working.

"Be careful," Winnie said as he headed back toward the front door.

"I will."

Rocket jogged back out to his truck and headed down the street toward the small convenience store at the entrance to Winnie's neighborhood. There were a few cars in the lot, and he saw Winnie's old Buick.

He climbed out and headed for the door, excited to see the look of surprise—and probably a bit of irritation—on Jayme's face when she saw him. He knew she loved when he looked after her, but even he could admit that not waiting for her to get back from the store was going a little overboard. In his defense though, he was anxious for their four-day staycation to start. He'd been looking forward to having her all to himself for weeks and was a bit resentful of being cheated out of some of his time with her because of work.

He was thinking about Jayme's reaction to seeing him as he opened the door to the small convenience store, and therefore was a little slow in realizing what was going on.

Three men, dressed all in black, turned to stare at him as he entered. One was holding a pistol on the teenager behind the counter. Another was standing near a group of customers in one of the aisles, and the third was farther back, standing near Jayme and the cold case.

The men looked young, probably in their late

teens or early twenties. They had bandanas over their faces but weren't wearing gloves.

"Shit!" the guy in the aisle swore.

Rocket was moving before he consciously thought about it. He had eyes for only one person. The man with the gun standing near Jayme. The guy at the counter was closer, but he didn't even think about trying to tackle him. He ducked behind a counter and headed for Jayme. It was stupid. He knew it was. But something in his brain had short circuited. His only thought was getting to the woman he loved.

A gunshot rang out, and screams sounded loud in the small store. There was more swearing and the sound of shelves being knocked over and items falling to the floor. But Rocket didn't look around, he was still focused on getting to Jayme.

He came around the back of the aisle and stared at the punk near Jayme. He'd turned toward the group of women toward the front of the store who were screaming. From what Rocket could see, the group had actually jumped one of the would-be robbers. An alarm blared through the store, obviously set off by the clerk. The third gunman yelled, "fuck this," then took off running for the door.

Everything in the store was in complete chaos, and the last thing Rocket wanted was the gunman nearest Jayme to start shooting his weapon to try to gain control. Just as he had the thought, the man lifted his hand, the one holding the weapon.

Rocket's heart nearly stopped beating in his chest when he turned toward Jayme. His hand was shaking as if he was scared to death. But before Rocket could act, a flash of light appeared from the muzzle of the pistol.

Then Rocket was on him. They both slammed to the hard tile floor and the pistol went skittering away as the young man lost his grip. Without hesitation, Rocket punched him once. Then twice. Then a third time. The man had dared to hold a weapon toward Jayme. He'd shot at her. No one did that and got away with it. Not on his watch.

The man beneath him fought back, but was no match for Rocket's size, strength, and anger.

"Rocket! Stop! He's down."

The words barely registered. Rocket's adrenaline was coursing through his veins and he couldn't get the look of absolute fright on Jayme's face out of his mind.

It wasn't until he felt a hand on the side of his face, a touch he recognized at a soul deep level, that he stopped, his fist half-cocked and ready to slam down into the asshole's face once more.

"Rocket, I'm okay. We're all okay."

Looking up, Rocket saw his Jayme staring at him with a mixture of concern and terror on her face.

That did it. He turned away from the punk, now unconscious on the floor, and hauled Jayme into him. She came without hesitation. Without a second thought. Pressing against him as if she could burrow into his skin and become one with him.

He lifted a knee and shuffled to the side of the man he'd beaten and fell onto his ass, still holding Jayme to him.

"I'm okay," she mumbled into his neck. "I'm okay."

Rocket couldn't speak. Could barely see. All he could do was feel. Things could've gone so differently. His own actions could've gotten Jayme killed. But he couldn't *not* run toward her. He'd almost been too late. He could've lost her before they'd even begun to live their lives together.

Vaguely, Rocket heard people moving around him. Someone found some rope and tied up the man he'd subdued. Someone else was on a phone with 9-1-1. But Rocket still couldn't move. It was as if he were paralyzed. Blinking, he saw the glass of the cold case had shattered and was in pieces on the floor around them. A woman was crying hysterically nearby and being comforted by another customer. It was chaos... and all he could do was sit where he was and feel

Jayme's heart beating against his chest. He'd never felt anything better in all his life.

When Rocket had been in the Navy, he'd experienced times when he was scared. There were a few times when the ship he was on had been locked down because of the threat of incoming missiles, but in the end, nothing had ever happened. But that didn't mean the fear hadn't been intense when they were waiting for the all clear.

But he'd never been as scared as he'd been a minute ago. Seeing Jayme on the receiving end of the muzzle of a gun had been the most frightened he'd ever been in his life. He couldn't live without her. Now that he'd found her, Rocket knew without a doubt that losing her would make him a shell of the man. She was his better half, and he damn well knew it.

"Rocket?" He heard her say his name, but all he could do was shake his head and bury his nose harder into the velvety skin between her shoulder and neck. Her thick hair tickled his face, but he didn't care.

"You're hurting me," she whispered.

He immediately loosened his grasp and pulled back to look at her. It was the only thing she could've said that would've made him let go. He'd never hurt her. He'd rather die first.

The first thing he saw was that her pupils were

dilated to twice their usual size. Her face was white, and she was frowning. Then he saw the blood. It wasn't a lot, but there was a small stream of bright red blood oozing down the side of her temple. "You're bleeding," he whispered, knowing he was probably in shock.

Jayme lifted a hand to wipe her face, but Rocket caught it before she could touch herself.

"Is it bad?" she asked.

"No." It wasn't, but still, seeing even a drop of Jayme's blood was horrifying.

"I think when the case shattered, some of the glass must've hit me," she said softly.

"You weren't shot?" Rocket asked, belatedly realizing that should've been the first thing he did... check her for serious injuries.

"No. At least I don't think so."

Rocket immediately began to run his hands over her body, checking for gunshot wounds. When she didn't flinch away from his touch, and he didn't find any more blood, he breathed out a sigh of relief.

"Are you all right?" she asked.

"Me?" he said in confusion.

She picked up one of his hands and held it gently. "Your poor hands," she said softly.

Rocket didn't give a shit about the condition of his hands. As far as he was concerned, he'd wear his scrapes and bruises with pride. Besides, his hands were always nicked and beaten up because of his job. Not to mention stained with the oil he was constantly getting all over them at the garage.

"Nobody move!" a harsh voice ordered from near the door.

Turning his head, Rocket saw a police officer standing just inside the door with his weapon drawn.

Taking a deep breath, he did his best to get control of his body and mind once more. Jayme was all right. As was he. It would take some time for the officers to figure out what had gone down tonight, but he had no doubt the videos would exonerate him for nearly killing the man still lying unconscious nearby.

Jayme was safe. Nothing else mattered.

EPILOGUE

Christmas Day

Jayme woke up on December twenty-fifth and sighed in contentment. She was wrapped tightly in Rocket's arms, just as she'd been when she went to sleep. They'd both been a bit clingy for the last two days, which was all right with her. Memaw had also been hit hard by what had almost happened.

Jayme knew she'd never forget the look on Rocket's face as he ran toward the young man with the gun nearest to her. He was one hundred percent focused on getting to the man and preventing him from hurting her. Of course, there was no way he could've prevented a bullet from hitting her; luckily the shot had gone wide and had hit the cold case behind her instead of tearing through her flesh.

Seeing Rocket beat the man into unconsciousness should've turned her off. The violence should've freaked her out, but what had scared her instead was how hard it had been to get Rocket to stop.

They both had a kind of post-traumatic stress disorder from the robbery, and she knew it would take a while for either of them to feel safe shopping anywhere again. And Jayme had a feeling Rocket wasn't going to let her go into any gas stations or convenience stores anytime soon. But that was all right with her. She wasn't too keen on the idea herself.

They'd spent Christmas Eve with Memaw and would be heading back over to her house today. Her grandmother needed the reassurance of her presence, and honestly, Jayme needed her memaw's presence as well.

"Good morning," Rocket said softly. "Merry Christmas."

"Merry Christmas," she told him softly. She didn't pull out of his arms, but tilted her head up so she could see his eyes. She watched as his gaze roamed her face then over her shoulders, as if he was visually inspecting her to make sure she was all right.

"How do you feel this morning?" he asked.

"I'm good. How are *you*? How do your hands feel?" She'd been dismayed to see his hands scraped up and bruised, but he'd merely shrugged and told her that they'd heal soon enough.

"They're fine," he told her, smoothing a piece of hair behind her ear.

Jayme had always loved his hands. He'd admitted that he was extremely self-conscious about them, because they were usually stained with oil. But the calluses he hated felt amazing against her bare skin, and the fact that he could palm her ass cheeks with those hands and hold her up while he took her against a wall, or on the counter, or anywhere else, made her shiver with delight.

And now she knew he'd do whatever it took to protect her with those hands as well.

Taking one gently, she kissed the palm before holding it to her cheek and giving him the weight of her head.

"I love you," Rocket said.

"I love you too. What's the plan for today?" she asked.

"I told Winnie we'd be over for lunch," Rocket said.

Jayme nodded. "She claims not to like presents, but she does."

"Sounds like someone else I know," Rocket said with a grin.

Jayme could only smile back. It was true. She loved presents. Didn't matter what they were. Rocket could wrap up a fork and she'd be happy. But judging by the pile of presents under the tree downstairs, he'd gone overboard.

He pulled away from her to reach into the drawer next to his side of the bed, then rolled back over to face her.

He was holding a small black velvet box.

Jayme looked from the box to his eyes in surprise. "What's this?"

"I've had this for months. I was trying to come up with the perfect time to give it to you. I wanted to give you a story you could tell our kids and grandkids that would blow them away and make them think their dad and grandfather was the shit. But after what happened, I'm not willing to wait one second longer. So I have no extravagant gestures, no balloons, no flash mob singing some sappy song. I'm just a man who's madly in love with you, and who doesn't want to wait to make you his in every way possible."

Jayme's heart nearly stopped in her chest when he opened the small box and continued.

"I've waited my whole life for you, Jayme Cald-well. I love you more than you'll ever know. Will you marry me? Have children with me? I know this is an insane time for you with your bakery opening in a week, but life is never guaranteed, I think we both learned that after what happened."

Jayme's eyes filled with tears. "I don't need any huge gestures. I just need you. Yes, of course I'll marry you!"

She was already lying next to him, but she threw herself into his arms as best she could anyway, laughing with happiness as he grunted and caught her. He rolled until she was under him, and Jayme could feel his erection against her thigh. He fumbled with the box but eventually got the ring out. Jayme held her hand up, and he slid the most beautiful ring she'd ever seen down her finger.

Turning her hand in an age old gesture, Jayme looked at the ring Rocket had bought for her. It was classy, yet untraditional.

"Do you like it?" Rocket asked.

Hearing the trepidation in his tone, Jayme nodded enthusiastically. "Like it? Those words are way too tame for how I feel about this ring. I love it. It's the most beautiful thing I've ever seen!" she gushed.

"I wanted to get you something that you didn't have to take off while you were cooking or rolling dough. I know it's a little different than usual engagement rings, and I'm happy to exchange it for something you like better if you want."

"I couldn't like anything better than this ring, Rocket. It's perfect."

And it was. The platinum band was wide and flat; embedded in the metal were at least a half dozen diamonds, set so they didn't stick up from the band. It wouldn't matter if it spun on her finger while she was cooking or baking, it wouldn't get in her way. The diamonds wouldn't be able to get gunked up with flour, and she wouldn't have to worry about catching a stone on anything when she was in the kitchen. It was obvious Rocket had thought long and hard about the kind of ring that would work best for her profession. It just hammered home how well this man knew her.

And just like that, tears formed in her eyes and Jayme was crying.

"I hope those are happy tears," Rocket said a little nervously.

Jayme could only nod. She felt Rocket lower himself gently on top of her, and she buried her nose into the side of his neck. Eventually, she got herself together and looked up into the beautiful brown eyes of the man she loved more than she'd ever loved anyone before. "For the record, your proposal was perfect."

He smiled and shrugged. "We'll have to think of a good story to tell our kids. I'm not sure they'd be impressed with, 'We were naked and in bed when your father proposed.'"

Jayme chuckled. She loved how Rocket kept talking about their children. She'd always wanted kids, but had started to think they weren't in the cards for her. Now she couldn't think of anything but having Rocket's babies.

"But maybe they'll be more impressed when they hear that we picked up our marriage license the day after I popped the question...and had our ceremony the second the seventy-two hour waiting period was over."

Jayme was still thinking about having Rocket's children, so it took a second for his words to sink in. "What?"

"The courthouse is closed today, but I thought tomorrow we could go get our license. Unfortunately, Texas has a three-day waiting period though. How does the twenty-ninth sound for an anniversary date?"

Jayme was shocked. She blinked in surprise. "Seriously?"

"Yes," Rocket said, his gaze boring into hers. "The worst day of my life was when I walked into that store and realized what was happening. I knew I couldn't get to you in time if that man decided to shoot you. When I heard that gun go off, the only thing I could think about was what a dumbass I'd been for not making you mine sooner. It was a miracle that you weren't hit by that bullet, and I don't want to wait another second to start our lives together."

"We're already living together," Jayme said, not sure why she was even protesting.

"I want you to have my name...if you'll have it. I want to protect you legally and monetarily. I want you to know that you never have to worry about anything ever again. I'll take care of you and any children we might have. I'll never hurt you. I won't cheat. You're it for me, Jayme, and I don't want to wait a second longer than necessary to start our lives together."

How could she complain about that? "Memaw wants to walk me down the aisle," she warned.

"Of course. I'd never leave your grandmother out of our ceremony. She was the one who set us up in the first place. We can have a big ceremony later if you want, I just...I need you to be mine legally."

Jayme knew what had happened had hit Rocket hard, but she was just beginning to realize exactly *how* hard. "I don't need a big, expensive wedding. I just need you."

"We could invite your parents down," he started, but Jayme shook her head and put a finger over his lips.

"They'll understand. My mom will probably swoon with delight that you were so impatient to marry me that you wouldn't wait. We might need to have a reception or something so they can officially celebrate with us, but I don't think they'll mind that they missed the actual ceremony. I think they'll be happy I'm no longer an old maid."

"You'll never be an old maid," Rocket said without hesitation. "So, you're okay with us tying the knot this week?"

"Yes. I love you, Rocket. And you might've been worried about me in that store, but I was terrified for *you*. You interrupting their holdup could've made them start shooting at *you*. I think once they got everyone's money, they would've simply left without hurting us. But you startled them, those women attacked one of them, and all I could think about was one of them killing you. When you started running toward me, I swear I saw my life flash before my eyes. I'd marry you tomorrow if it was possible. And of course I want to take your name. I can't think of anything better than being Jayme Long."

"You're the best Christmas present I've ever received," Rocket said reverently.

"Same," Jayme told him.

"I know you're anxious to go downstairs and open all those presents you've been eyeballing and I haven't let you touch, squeeze, or shake...but maybe you'd be willing to wait another hour or so?" Rocket asked as his fingers began to play with one of her nipples.

And just like that, Jayme was wet. "I don't know..." she teased. "What did you have in mind?"

"I just need a morning snack," Rocket said as he slowly slid down her body, pushing the covers back as he went.

Smiling in contentment, Jayme opened her legs, giving him room. Her man was amazing with his mouth. "I suppose I can wait," she said on a dramatic sigh as he parted her folds and blew lightly on her clit.

"Good of you," Rocket said before lowering his head.

It was more than an hour before they'd climbed out of bed and got dressed, heading downstairs to celebrate their first Christmas together. And they were late getting over to her grandmother's house because after opening all her presents, and seeing how generous her fiancé was, Jayme had to demonstrate her gratitude and how much she loved him right there under the lights of their Christmas tree.

. . .

Fourteen months later

Rocket held Jayme's hand as she grunted and bore down once more.

"That's it. He's almost here!" the doctor said encouragingly.

Rocket wanted to hurt the young doctor. She'd been saying that for what seemed like hours.

He'd been so excited when Jayme had told him she was pregnant, but now, after seeing how difficult giving birth actually was and how much pain Jayme had been in for hours, he vowed not to put her through this ever again. Having one child was going to have to be enough.

"I see his head!" the doctor said excitedly. "Come here, Dad, and get ready."

Rocket pried his hand from Jayme's with reluctance and quickly moved to stand beside the doctor. Considering how long it took for his son to finally decide he was ready to enter the world, the next few minutes went by surprisingly fast. What looked like a slimy alien slipped out of his wife's body, and he cut the cord where the doctor instructed him to. Then their son was taken over to a table to be weighed and stimulated before he was cleaned up and handed to his mother.

Rocket went back to Jayme's side and wiped her brow as the doctor finished up between her legs.

"How is he?" Jayme asked anxiously. "Is he all right?"

Before Rocket could reassure her, they heard a loud, pissed-off wail come from the table their son had been placed on.

Jayme smiled weakly up at him.

"He's fine," Rocket told her unnecessarily. "And he's beautiful. I love you so much!"

A nurse brought their son over to Jayme. She placed him on her chest so they were skin-to-skin, and Jayme looked down at him and her eyes immediately filled with tears. "He's perfect!"

Rocket couldn't even respond. He *was* perfect. Their son was absolutely perfect. He wouldn't have cared what he looked like or if he'd had some sort of medical condition. He was theirs. So he was perfect. Rocket had never been happier.

Life over the last year or so hadn't been without its ups and downs. Warm Delights hadn't taken off immediately. It had been a hard first six months, but slowly word had gotten out about the newest bakery in town, and Jayme was finally seeing a healthy profit after all her sweat and tears.

Rocket had been given the opportunity to go overseas for his employer for six months. It would've meant doubling his salary, but they'd just found out Jayme was pregnant and he hadn't wanted to miss a second of it. So he'd declined...without discussing it with his wife.

Jayme was pissed at him for at least a week, before he'd finally sat her down and they'd hashed things out. She was upset he'd made such a big decision without even talking to her about it, and Rocket had a hard time understanding why she was mad when she agreed with his decision in the first place. But they'd worked through that, and their relationship had become stronger as a result.

"Welcome to the family, Connor Rocket Long," Jayme whispered.

Rocket's throat closed up and his eyes filled with tears. They'd had some heated conversations over the last few months about what to name their son, as well. Jayme had wanted to name him Rocket Junior, but there was no way Rocket was going to put his son through what he'd gone through when he was a kid. He'd been teased mercilessly. He wanted their son to have a nice, normal name, that no one would make fun of him for. He might get teased for other things, but at least it wouldn't be because of something Rocket could prevent.

So Jayme had relented on his first name, but still

insisted on giving him a part of his father, the man she loved more than life itself.

Their son yawned, opening his mouth wide and letting out a small squeak, before scrunching his eyes closed and sighing.

"Thank you," Rocket whispered.

"I think that's my line," Jayme whispered back, not wanting to wake their sleeping son.

"Nope. Thank you for giving me a chance. Thank you for loving me. Thank you for trusting me to treat you right. Thank you for wanting to have children with me. Just...thank you for sharing your life with me."

Now Jayme was crying. "You're welcome," she told him with a watery smile.

If someone had told him two years ago that he'd be where he was today, married, with a beautiful son, he would've rolled his eyes at them and told them they were crazy. He'd spent forty years looking for "the one," and he'd had no reason to believe he'd ever find her. But here she was.

Here they were.

"Come on, Dad, we've got to move your wife up to a room and we need to take little Connor back for some TLC," one of the nurses said.

Rocket straightened, but grabbed ahold of his wife's hand as they gently took Connor from her.

"They'll give him back," Jayme said with a small chuckle. When his eyes met hers, she said, "You were looking at him as if you'd never see him again."

"I just...he's a miracle, and I can't *stop* looking at him."

"You'll have plenty of time to do that in the next eighteen years," she said dryly, then yawned, much as their son had done.

Rocket mentally shook himself. Jayme had just been through the most amazing thing he'd ever seen in his life. She needed sleep, and food, and for him to get his head out of his ass and to take care of her. As soon as the nurses got her settled, he'd help her change into the nightgown they'd brought from home. She'd want the fuzzy blanket they'd brought as well. Then there was Winnie. She was going to want to see her granddaughter and great-grandson.

"What's that smile for?" Jayme asked.

"Just thinking about what Winnie's going to say when she sees Connor for the first time."

Husband and wife shared a smile. Winnie was still going strong at ninety-two and a half, and sometimes they thought she was more excited about this child than they were.

"Rocket?" Jayme asked.

"Yeah?"

"I love you."

"Love you too, sweetheart," Rocket said. Life was good. He was a damn lucky man...and he knew it.

Five years later

"Connor! Stop teasing your sister!" Jayme yelled from the kitchen. She was finishing up dinner and Rocket knew by the sound of her voice that she was at the end of her rope.

Their kids were awesome, but they were also quite a handful. They'd had Kayleigh one year almost to the day that they'd had Connor. They hadn't planned on having a second kid so close to the first, but they hadn't taken the necessary precautions after Jayme had been cleared to have sex again.

They'd talked about it, and Rocket had gladly agreed to having a vasectomy while Jayme had been pregnant with Kayleigh. The last thing he wanted was to put any more stress and strain on his wife, and since they both agreed that two kids seemed perfect for their family, it was a no-brainer.

Now they could make love without worrying about unintended consequences. He could fuck his wife without reservations...but of course, that was easier said than done. With two kids in the house, their life was hectic, but they always seemed to find time to connect physically and emotionally.

Connor was a rambunctious five-year-old who definitely took after his father. He was a big kid, and the doctors said he'd be a big adult, as well. Which wasn't exactly a surprise since Rocket was six-four himself. Connor hadn't quite learned his own strength yet, and they were working on that. But one thing that Rocket had done from the time he'd brought his son home was impress upon him the importance of looking after those who were smaller or weaker than himself. There was no way any son of Rocket's was going to be a bully. No way in hell.

Then there was Kayleigh. She was small, like her mom, which made Rocket smile every time he looked at her. She had gorgeous thick hair, which was in a tangle on her head more often than not. Her blue eyes could sway him as easily as her mom's too. Jayme accused him of spoiling her, but Rocket didn't care. That was his job as a father.

But Kayleigh was no shrinking violet. She was as rough and tumble as her older brother. Surprisingly, it was Connor who loved to spend hours in the kitchen with his mom, learning how to chop, stir, and bake, while Kayleigh would rather spend her time out in the garage with her daddy, learning the names of the tools he used and getting oil all over her hands.

"Kids!" Rocket yelled. "Come here!"

His son and daughter came running toward him, leaping into his lap and fighting over which knee they sat on.

"Calm down and I'll tell you a story," Rocket told them.

"Tell us about your wedding!" Connor insisted.

Rocket sighed. "Are you sure? You've heard that one a million times," Rocket said.

"Hush up and tell them," Winnie retorted from her chair.

They'd moved Jayme's grandmother in with them a year and a half ago. She hadn't wanted to leave her pretty little house, but it was time. She'd been having a hard time taking care of herself and needed some help. And neither Rocket nor Jayme could bear to put her in a nursing home or assisted living center. So Memaw was spending the last years of her life in their home. Surrounded by the craziness that was a house with two little kids and two working adults.

"Right, so your mom and I got engaged on Christmas Day. I gave her the beautiful ring she still wears today, and we immediately went to get the proper paperwork so we could tie the knot as soon as possible."

Connor and Kayleigh were enthralled, which

amused Rocket, since they'd heard this story so many times before.

"When the big day came, we went down to the courthouse with your memaw. She wanted to walk your mom down the aisle, since she was the one who'd introduced me to her. When we got there, though, things were crazy. Apparently a lot of other couples had the same idea as us, and it was getting later and later. The courthouse was going to close, and we were afraid we wouldn't be able to get married that day, which would've been a huge bummer because we'd been looking forward to it so much.

"Just when we didn't think it was going to happen, our names were called. So the three of us got up and went into the room. But instead of a beautifully decorated room, as we'd envisioned, we were led to a cubicle. There was no aisle, but your memaw was determined. She grabbed your mom's hand and pulled her away from me. She pushed me about three feet in front of them and ordered me to turn around.

"I was trying to keep my laughter to myself, but it was impossible. So I took a step away from your mom and Memaw lifted her chin and she and Jayme took one step toward me. Then Memaw put your mom's hand in mine and said, 'There. Done.'

"Both your mom and I were trying so hard not to laugh, but when the clerk started talking, it was impossible not to. He was going on about how 'we were gathered here today' when there was no 'we.' It was just us, your memaw, and two people peeking into the cubicle from the hall, who were the witnesses. And once we started giggling, we couldn't stop. The clerk didn't stop though, he kept talking over our giggles. By the time he got to the part where we were supposed to say our vows, all we could get out was, 'I do.' We couldn't say the beautiful vows we'd practiced!"

Both Connor and Kayleigh were laughing by then, and Rocket saw Jayme standing in the kitchen looking over at them with a huge smile on her face.

"But you guys had a do-over!" Connor said confidently.

"We did. We were officially married that day, December twenty-ninth, but three months later we had a party, right here in our own backyard, and we got to say the vows we'd made up for each other, and Memaw got to walk your mom down a more proper aisle."

"It was a big party!" Kayleigh piped in. "You invited all your friends from the Navy base and Mom made all the cookies!"

"That's right. Nana and Papa were there, as well as Grams and Grandpa."

Rocket loved that his kids wanted to hear the

story about their parents' wedding over and over. He shared a look with Jayme from across the room. Their wedding hadn't turned out as they'd expected, but the story from that day never failed to make them smile, and as far as he was concerned, that was a gift.

"Dinner's ready," Jayme called out.

Connor and Kayleigh bounded from his lap and ran to the table. They all didn't eat together every night, but did so as often as they could.

Rocket stood and helped Winnie to her feet. When he got her settled at the table, he went into the kitchen. He took a quick second to kiss his wife. "Thanks for dinner."

He never took her for granted. She always did her best to get home at a reasonable time, never forgetting what he'd told her once upon a time, that he loved coming home to the smell of dinner cooking.

"You're welcome," Jayme said.

Then Rocket leaned down and nuzzled the side of her neck, never getting tired of his wife's soft moans and how she always grabbed on to him as if she couldn't help herself. "I'll show you how appreciative I am tonight."

Her swift intake of breath made him smile.

"Mom! I'm hungry!" Kayleigh exclaimed from the table.

"Your offspring is hungry," Jayme said, as she reached for a plate she'd already made up and shoved it into Rocket's hands.

Grinning, Rocket took it. But before he headed to the table to feed his monsters, he took the time to kiss Jayme's forehead gently. They'd been married for over six years, and he loved her even more than he did when he'd first put his ring on her finger.

He didn't know what was in store for the next six years, but he couldn't wait to find out.

Twenty years later

"Merry Christmas," Rocket told Jayme as he handed her a small box. This was their tradition, had been ever since that first Christmas together. They'd wake up Christmas morning and he'd give her a present.

"You spoil me," she told him softly.

"Yup," Rocket agreed.

He watched as she opened the long box and exclaimed in delight at the knife that was inside.

"You got me that knife set I wanted!" she exclaimed.

"Nope. Just one. Those things were expensive," Rocket teased.

But Jayme shook her head and laughed. "Whatever. You wouldn't get me just one knife. I know you."

She did. Rocket kissed her. "The rest are downstairs waiting to be opened. And you should know, you're the only woman I'd ever consider giving a set of wicked sharp knives to."

Jayme chuckled. "Yeah, well, if I haven't killed you yet, I think you're safe." She put the knife back in the box and snuggled into his side. "Remember when the kids were young and you'd have to set the alarm for like three in the morning so we could have our special moment without being interrupted?"

Rocket nodded. "Yeah. Our kids had a knack for waking up at the butt crack of dawn and pouncing on us."

They were both quiet for a moment, then Jayme said, "I miss that."

"Well, by the time they were teenagers, they were happy to have a day to sleep in. It was *us* going in to wake *them* up when they still weren't awake by nine," Rocket mused.

"True. They've turned out pretty good, haven't they?" Jayme asked.

They had. Connor had inherited his mom's love of cooking and had gone to culinary school. He was working at a five-star restaurant up in Dallas and had dreams of opening his own restaurant one day. Rocket was somewhat upset on Jayme's behalf that Connor hadn't wanted to take over her bakery, but Jayme reassured him she was happy he was taking his own path in life. She'd finally decided to sell Warm Delights, and seemed happy that her legacy would continue on.

Kayleigh had taken after Rocket, getting her associate's degree in automotive technology, and had been hired on by the very same contractor Rocket had retired from. She was working at Fort Bragg, North Carolina. Currently, both their kids were home for an entire week.

"They're amazing," Rocket said, his voice full of pride.

Jayme looked over at the clock. "It's seven. Think we should go in and make them get up now?"

Rocket pretended to think about it before shaking his head. "We've got two hours of peace, at least. I can think of better things to do than torture our children."

"Yeah?" Jayme asked. "I *could* use some more sleep."

Their sex life had been robust over the years, but they no longer needed or wanted to be intimate every night. Both were content to merely snuggle and hold each other as they slept. But every now and then, the need for more struck them. Like now.

Rocket reached for the hem of the tank top Jayme was wearing and slipped his hand under it. "Sleep, huh?"

She squirmed against him. "Okay, maybe I'm not *that* tired," she teased.

Rocket grinned and scooted down her body, grabbing hold of the panties she had on as he went. He might be in his mid-sixties, but he'd never get enough of his wife. He loved her taste, how she bucked against him, and how she said his name when she came. Hell, Rocket loved everything about Jayme.

Two hours later, after waking up their kids, and after Jayme had served the biggest, gooiest cinnamon rolls that she knew her family loved, Rocket watched as his family opened their Christmas gifts.

"Did you get everything you wanted?" Jayme asked when the gifts had been opened. There was wrapping paper everywhere, and the house was a mess.

Rocket turned to his wife and kissed her temple, holding her tighter against his side. "I got everything I wanted twenty-six years ago when you said 'I do,'" he told her honestly.

Sometimes Rocket had flashbacks to that time when he'd walked into an armed robbery and saw his wife on the wrong end of a gun, and all he could do was thank his lucky stars that they'd both come out of it alive. He couldn't imagine not having Connor or Kayleigh in his life. Couldn't imagine not living the life he'd lived for the last twenty-six years.

"I love you," Jayme said.

"I love you too," Rocket returned.

Their life had its share of ups and downs, but he wouldn't change one thing about it. Not one single thing.

Next up in the series is Oz and Riley's story in *Shielding Riley*. Oz has suddenly found himself the guardian of his ten year old nephew and is way out of his element. Luckily, his neighbor, Riley, is there to help him figure things out. But of course life is full of ups and downs, and when a secret comes to light, Oz has to fight for what he wants...a family.

Haven't read Memaw's neighbors, Brain and Aspen? Pick up *Shielding Aspen* today!

Also by Susan Stoker

Delta Team Two Series
Shielding Gillian
Shielding Kinley
Shielding Aspen
Shielding Jayme (novella)
Shielding Riley (Jan 2021)
Shielding Devyn (May 2021)
Shielding Ember (Sep 2021)
Shielding Sierra (TBA)

SEAL of Protection Series
Protecting Caroline
Protecting Alabama
Protecting Fiona
Marrying Caroline (novella)
Protecting Summer
Protecting Cheyenne
Protecting Jessyka
Protecting Julie (novella)
Protecting Melody
Protecting the Future
Protecting Kiera (novella)
Protecting Alabama's Kids (novella)
Protecting Dakota

SEAL of Protection: Legacy Series

Securing Caite

Securing Brenae (novella)

Securing Sidney

Securing Piper

Securing Zoey

Securing Avery

Securing Kalee

Securing Jane (Feb 2021)

SEAL Team Hawaii Series

Finding Elodie (Apr 2021)

Finding Lexie (Aug 2021)

Finding Kenna (Oct 2021)

Finding Monica (TBA)

Finding Carly (TBA)

Finding Ashlyn (TBA)

Finding Jodelle (TBA)

Delta Force Heroes Series

Rescuing Rayne

Rescuing Aimee (novella)

Rescuing Emily

Rescuing Harley

Marrying Emily (novella)

Rescuing Kassie

Rescuing Bryn

Rescuing Casey
Rescuing Sadie (novella)
Rescuing Wendy
Rescuing Mary
Rescuing Macie (novella)

Badge of Honor: Texas Heroes Series

Justice for Mackenzie
Justice for Mickie
Justice for Corrie
Justice for Laine (novella)
Shelter for Elizabeth
Justice for Boone
Shelter for Adeline
Shelter for Sophie
Justice for Erin
Justice for Milena
Shelter for Blythe
Justice for Hope
Shelter for Quinn
Shelter for Koren
Shelter for Penelope

Ace Security Series

Claiming Grace
Claiming Alexis
Claiming Bailey

ALSO BY SUSAN STOKER

Claiming Felicity
Claiming Sarah

Mountain Mercenaries Series
Defending Allye
Defending Chloe
Defending Morgan
Defending Harlow
Defending Everly
Defending Zara
Defending Raven

Silverstone Series
Trusting Skylar
Trusting Taylor (Mar 2021)
Trusting Molly (July 2021)
Trusting Cassidy (Dec 2021)

Stand Alone
The Guardian Mist
Nature's Rift
A Princess for Cale
A Moment in Time- A Collection of Short Stories
Lambert's Lady

Special Operations Fan Fiction
http://www.AcesPress.com

ALSO BY SUSAN STOKER

Beyond Reality Series
Outback Hearts
Flaming Hearts
Frozen Hearts

Writing as Annie George:
Stepbrother Virgin (erotic novella)

ABOUT THE AUTHOR

New York Times, *USA Today* and *Wall Street Journal* Bestselling Author Susan Stoker has a heart as big as the state of Tennessee where she lives, but this all American girl has also spent the last fourteen years living in Missouri, California, Colorado, Indiana, and Texas. She's married to a retired Army man who now gets to follow *her* around the country.

She debuted her first series in 2014 and quickly followed that up with the SEAL of Protection Series, which solidified her love of writing and creating stories readers can get lost in.

If you enjoyed this book, or any book, please consider leaving a review. It's appreciated by authors more than you'll know.

www.stokeraces.com
www.AcesPress.com
susan@stokeraces.com

facebook.com/authorsusanstoker

twitter.com/Susan_Stoker

instagram.com/authorsusanstoker

goodreads.com/SusanStoker

bookbub.com/authors/susan-stoker

amazon.com/author/susanstoker

CPSIA information can be obtained
at www.ICGtesting.com
Printed in the USA
LVHW051652211220
674801LV00015B/2497

9 781644 991206